FAMILY OF SPIES

PARIS

A NOVEL

JODI CARMICHAEL

yellow dog

Yellow Dog
(an imprint of Great Plains Publications)
1173 Wolseley Avenue
Winnipeg, MB R3G 1H1
www.greatplains.mb.ca

Great Plains Publications gratefully acknowledges the financial support
provided for its publishing program by the Government of Canada
through the Canada Book Fund; the Canada Council for the Arts;
the Province of Manitoba through the Book Publishing Tax Credit
and the Book Publisher Marketing Assistance Program; and the
Manitoba Arts Council.

Design & Typography by Relish New Brand Experience
Interior illustrations by Jamie Gatta
Printed in Canada by Friesens

LIBRARY AND ARCHIVES CANADA CATALOGUING IN PUBLICATION

Carmichael, Jodi, author
    Family of spies / Jodi Carmichael.

Issued in print and electronic formats.
ISBN 978-1-927855-94-2 (softcover).--ISBN 978-1-927855-95-9 (EPUB).--
ISBN 978-1-927855-96-6 (Kindle)

    1. Title.

PS8605.A7559F36 2018   jC813'.6   C2017-907261-7
                                            C2017-907262-5

ENVIRONMENTAL BENEFITS STATEMENT

Great Plains Publications saved the following
resources by printing the pages of this book on
chlorine free paper made with 100% post-consumer
waste.

TREES	WATER	ENERGY	SOLID WASTE	GREENHOUSE GASES
7	3,186	3	213	588
FULLY GROWN	GALLONS	MILLION BTUs	POUNDS	POUNDS

Environmental impact estimates were made using the Environmental Paper Network
Paper Calculator32. For more information visit www.papercalculator.org.

Canada

FSC
www.fsc.org
MIX
Paper from
responsible sources
FSC® C016245

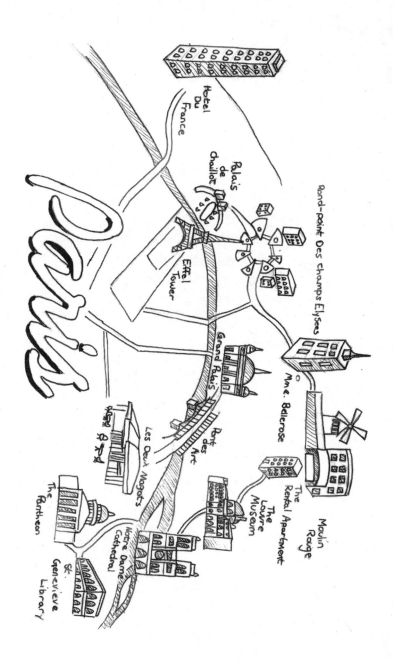

CHAPTER 1

Patience.

Ford MacKenzie had left all of his on the plane, along with several chocolate bar wrappers, an empty pack of mints, and—he patted his pockets—half a pack of gum.

He bounced on his toes, peering around the tired travellers in front of him. Another wicket opened and the line inched forward.

Ford's fingers drummed on his thighs. "This line is taking forever."

"Ah, patience. It is a virtuuuuuue," his mother sang.

How could Mom be so chill when right on the other side of the burly border guard was the Great European Adventure his parents had talked about for the past year? Ford sighed. "I want this vacation to start already."

"No need to rush it. Live in the moment, Ford. Our holiday will be marvell-ooooooous!" She trilled the word until it warbled around the room and over the heads of the people in line. It soared right to the security guard who stood at attention next to the middle wicket. The man stared at Ford's mother and frowned. He pulled a slip of paper from his front lapel pocket and scribbled something on it.

Ford slumped into his hoodie. He knew that look. His brother Gavin caught his eye and mouthed, "Not again." At least they had that in common—basic parental embarrassment.

"*Prochain*," the customs agent at the far side of the room called. Finally, their turn. The security guard ambled over to the agent's booth and whispered something to her.

His mom rolled an overstuffed carry-on bag plastered with Canadian flag stickers behind her. She nearly skipped towards the clerk. "Come along ma' boy-os," she crooned.

His dad's nose was buried in his dictionary. "*Attendez-moi, mes enfants*," he said. His smile covered his entire long, thin face, blue eyes burned with excitement behind his glasses. "How'd I do?"

"Well—" Gavin began.

Ford interrupted his brother. "Great, Dad. That was perfect." It was a lie. Dad got the words right but it sounded more like some alien language than French.

"This waaaay," Mom warbled.

As Ford stepped behind her, he heard the guard whisper to the customs agent, "*Une Canadienne folle*." Crazy Canadian.

They weren't even officially in France and already the French had his parents figured out. Heat rushed up Ford's neck and burned across his face in seconds.

Yup. My parents are beyond plain weird. They're nuts.

CHAPTER 2

"May Day!" Ford's Aunt June called as she sprinted across the airport towards them. Red curls bounced in every direction.

"June Bug!" His mom sang to her twin. His mom dropped her bag and raced through the crowd, tripping over an elderly man's cane but not slowing.

Ford's dad stuffed his dictionary under his arm, gathered her bag, and followed his wife, smiling. Gavin made a beeline for the drink machine, looking as embarrassed as Ford felt. Ford searched the crowd for his cousin, Ellie. She was the only other normal person in their family. Well, maybe above normal when it came to brain activity, but at least she wasn't eccentric like the rest of them. He caught a glimpse of her long, black, curly hair when a huge arm wrapped itself around his shoulders, nearly knocking him over.

"Uncle Jim!" Ford said, regaining his balance. Uncle Jim loved surprises and his jokes were legendary, but not in the way he probably intended—they were more lame than ingenious.

Uncle Jim's dark cheeks dimpled as his smile creased around his eyes, and he tightened his one-armed bear hug. Ford couldn't take a deep breath. Finally, Uncle

Jim released him and Ford staggered, sucking in air. He thumped Ford on the back and marched towards Ford's parents.

His family made an embarrassingly loud ruckus. He sighed. At least they were impossible to lose in a crowd. Gavin was stuck in the midst of the chaos, looking like a younger version of Dad. Same dark hair, same dark glasses and, just like Dad, not one single freckle. Unlike Ford. One day, Ford was sure, his freckles would cover every inch of his body. Gavin glanced at Ford. He looked like he wished he was back on campus. Ford took a step towards them, but stopped as his brother disappeared into Uncle Jim's infamous bear hug. No way was he going in for another round of crushing embraces.

"Ford!" Ellie said, her voice bubbling. He turned just as she threw an armload of maps and pamphlets to the ground and bear-hugged him. Thankfully, she wasn't as strong as Uncle Jim. Her thick hair flew around his shoulders like a shawl. The best thing about Ellie, in Ford's opinion, was you always knew what she was feeling. Happy, sad, furious—she let you know.

She pulled away and hooted with her fist pumped high. "Now, our vacation can begin!"

Ford smiled, but he wasn't nearly as joyous as his cousin. "I wish it was just the two of us. Gavin is here."

"Yeah, I heard, but why is that a problem?"

"It isn't. I guess, it's just..."

Ford wasn't sure how to put into words how he felt about being completely out-IQed when he was around the two of them. Sometimes he felt like such an outsider, especially when they got talking about subjects he knew nothing about, like quantum physics or calculus. Ford sighed. It was like they spoke a foreign language when they got together.

"Just...never mind."

Ellie frowned, then shrugged. "All right. Help me pick this stuff up." She knelt and gathered the pamphlets and brochures that lay scattered around her suitcases.

"How many bags did you bring?" Ford had crammed everything he needed for the summer into one suitcase and his backpack only contained his laptop, phone, and passport.

"A lady can never be too prepared."

"When did you become a lady?'

She walloped him again, this time on his thigh. Her knuckles dug deep.

"Charlie horse!" he cried. "*What the...*"

Ford swatted at her shoulder, but she jumped out of reach, laughing.

"Sucka," she drawled as she jogged backwards towards their family.

Ford scooped up the one pamphlet she'd forgotten. The words "Tourism France" splashed across a montage of photos of cafés, museums, and art galleries in Paris. An old black-and-white picture of a café caught his attention. There was something familiar about the place. As Ford ran his finger over the snapshot, a fleeting moment of déjà vu passed through him. He felt as if he'd been there, but that was impossible. He'd never been to France before.

"Weird," he muttered. He must have seen this photo or one just like it on the internet when they were planning their holiday. Or maybe he was just too impatient to start exploring France and in his mind he was already walking Parisian streets.

He stared at the small picture, trying to decipher the name of the café from the awning. All that was legible was the final word: *Magots*. What did that mean in English? Maggots? Ick. No, that couldn't be right. *Who'd eat at a maggot restaurant?*

"Hey! Slowpoke! Are you coming?" Ellie called.

"Wait up!" Ford tossed the glossy pamphlet into a trash can. Surely Ellie wouldn't miss just one.

CHAPTER 3

The taxi driver blared the horn as they wove through crowded Paris streets towards their holiday apartment. Ford jostled in the backseat, squished next to his brother and the window. Cafés, flower shops, and fruit stands flew past. He sat up straighter and pressed his fingers against the glass.

"Kids!" Dad shouted from the front seat. "The Eiffel Tower!"

That same strange déjà vu feeling nagged at him. Probably everyone felt that way when they saw the Eiffel Tower for the first time in person.

Gavin reached across him and pointed. "As you can see from the buildings around us, the architectural stylings are obviously eighteenth century."

"Obviously," Ford said, not even trying to keep the sarcasm from his voice. Architectural stylings? He was almost certain that Gavin had a computer inside his skull instead of a human brain. How could any real live sixteen-year-old know so many boring facts about so much boring stuff? It was surprising they were related.

The cab driver squealed around one last corner and screeched to a halt outside a stone-faced apartment building. Black, wrought-iron Juliet balconies dotted all five stories.

"Welcome to the … ninth… *arron…disse…ment*," Mom yodelled next to him. "The Annual MacKenzie-Whitaker Family Holiday begins!"

"*Oh mon dieu*," the cabbie muttered.

Ford's family clambered onto the street, hauling suitcases from the trunk and piling them high on the sidewalk. Ellie's taxi stopped only inches from where he stood and blasted its horn. Startled, he tumbled over the luggage and slammed his hip and elbow onto the pavement, still holding tight to his phone.

Ellie jumped from the cab while Uncle Jim unloaded their luggage and Aunt June snapped pictures of the buildings, the sidewalk, the trees, the cabbie, Uncle Jim; everything. She raced to Ford's side. Her shadow blocked the noonday sun. "What are you doing lying there? We have all of Paris to explore."

"I almost got run over."

"Yeah, but almost doesn't count." She extended one slender, tawny arm to him.

Ford batted her hand away and stood, stuffing his phone into his back pocket. He slung his bag firmly onto his shoulders and looked over at Gavin. Mom was draping duffle bags across him like a pack mule. Ford huffed and shook his head. It wouldn't matter if Ford carried all their bags from now until eternity, he would never be their favourite. He lunged at Ellie, who broke into laughter, easily dodging away.

She sprinted through the front doors of the apartment block and up the staircase. Ford chased after her, never slowing and taking the stairs two at a time. He gained on her as they approached the second floor.

Ellie sped down the hall, panting hard. She pointed to a charcoal grey door. "Apartment 210. It's our Home Sweet Home, or should I say *Maison Sucre Maison?*" She pulled a large silver key from her backpack.

"How did you get a key?" Ford asked.

"My scatterbrained parental units have entrusted me with all the 'Important and Official Items' on this trip. This includes the apartment key. They can't be trusted. Do you know how many times my mother has lost her cell phone? And my dad, he's even worse. For an actual genius, he forgets the most basic things, like where he parked his car and every single dentist appointment. I bet his mouth is full of cavities."

"I wonder if my parents will give me a key, too," Ford said. For sure they'd give one to Gavin.

Ellie shrugged and opened the door. "Honey, we're home!" she called, searching the walls for a light switch, which she found behind the open door. The dim hallway brightened. Ellie gasped.

CHAPTER 4

"Wow! This place is amazing," Ford said as they entered their apartment.

Honey-coloured herringbone wood floors zig-zagged the length of the twenty-foot-long hallway. Three bedrooms opened along each side of the corridor with a large living room at the end.

"Look at this!" Ellie pointed to a wicker basket on the hall table. It was stuffed with fruit, chocolates, coffees, cookies, and a dozen pamphlets and maps of Paris. Ellie pulled out the tourism brochures. "I didn't need to get any at the airport after all." She read the inside of one out loud in perfect French. She spoke better French than Ford did, and she wasn't even in French-immersion school. Heck, she wasn't even Canadian! Ford tried hard not to be jealous, but it wasn't always easy having a genius for a cousin. Ellie got their great-grandfather's Einstein-smart brain and she was almost as smart as Gavin. Ford, on the other hand, didn't get any of E.H. Crawford's infamous brilliance. He only inherited his great-grandfather's last name as his first and Ford knew, without a doubt, that he was merely average.

Ellie laid the brochures on the table and grabbed a large chocolate bar, ripped the wrapper off, and took a bite. "This is delicious."

"What else is in there?" Ford asked.

He elbowed Ellie out of the way and reached into the basket, but his gaze was drawn to the table and the scattered brochures. He pulled one from the pile. It was the maggot restaurant from the brochure at the airport. Ford laid it back on the table and, as he turned to follow Ellie, a prickle of déjà vu passed through him, drawing him back to the pamphlet. He ran his finger over the snapshot. His vision blurred. The pamphlet faded away and a cup of coffee flickered into focus. Ford yanked his hand away as steam laced with a nutty aroma tickled his nose.

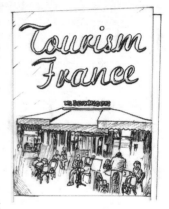

What the heck?

"Hey! Slowpoke! Don't stand there all day. I want to see the rest of the apartment," Ellie called.

Ford's head popped up. She was already down the hall. He looked back to the coffee cup, but it had disappeared. Only a faint coffee smell remained. He shook his head and blinked. Hallucinating coffee? He really needed sleep. He stuffed the glossy pamphlet to the bottom of the basket. Hopefully their parents wouldn't see it. Ford had no intention of eating bugs for breakfast.

"I call this one." Ellie stood in the doorway of the second bedroom, chomping on the chocolate bar. The room was small with a twin bed and a white bedspread embroidered with large, pink flowers. Fluffy white and lavender pillows were stacked high against the dark wood headboard. Large doors opened to a tiny balcony.

Ford entered the next room. It also had a single bed, but the bedspread was plain and light grey. Not one single flower. Perfect for him.

"Kids!" Ford's dad called from the hallway. His deep voice interrupted their excitement.

Ford grabbed his backpack and dumped its contents across the bed as Ellie stepped into his room.

"What are you doing?" she asked.

"I have to claim this room fast or Gavin might get it," he explained.

"Ford! Ellie! Come help us with the...baaaa-gaaaaage," sang Ford's mom.

"Hey Mom, where do you want the suitcases?" Gavin's voice rang through the apartment.

Ford and Ellie stood in his bedroom doorway and watched their family hustle through the apartment. Gavin stumbled down the hallway with a large suitcase in each hand, in addition to the bags slung crisscross across his shoulders. Ford sighed. Did Gavin purposely have to show him up?

"Over there," Mom said, directing Gavin to the far end of the hall.

Dad squeezed Gavin's shoulder. "This holiday is going to be *très, très perfecto mundo*."

"You've got your French mixed up with Italian again. I can give you some pointers if you want," Gavin offered.

Ford rolled his eyes and mumbled, "Of course you can, perfect son."

Ellie pinched his elbow. "Shut it."

Gavin dropped the bags and Mom gave him a big hug. "So great to have you here with us. We missed you this year." She looked at Ford. "You raced away so fast, you missed our impromptu photo session. But no worries, there will be plenty of time for family selfies."

Ford grimaced. Family selfies? Why did she talk like that?

"Isn't it great having your brother home from university and with us in Paris? We're all toooo-gether again, my sons, my sons," she sang, her eyes shining with tears.

"Yeah, great," mumbled Ford.

Dad tiptoed past them and winked at Ford as he inched toward the doorway. "Going to grab more bags," he called and darted out of the apartment.

"Do you remember the time—" Mom began.

"I think I hear Dad calling," Gavin said, and he dashed into the hallway before she could begin her walk down memory lane.

"Oh, okay. Maybe later. Ford, why don't you and Ellie sort the baggage into piles?" She pointed to the growing mountain of luggage that blocked much of the hallway.

Ford eyed the bags. An old, stained, beige brief-case sat on the floor next to Mom. It looked familiar.

"Whose is that?" A wave of nausea circled his belly. Maybe he shouldn't have eaten that beef burrito on the plane.

"It belonged to Great-Granddad Crawford."

"Great-Granddad? Really? Cool." Ford stepped closer.

Mom smiled and patted the leather side. "I guess you could call it a family heirloom. It contains all sorts of papers from his war years. History is in there. You know, your great-grand-father was not just any old air force pilot from Newfoundland. He was a Rhodes Scholar." Her eyes grew glassy. "My mom was always so proud of him. I thought it would be fun to have it with us—to see Paris from his point of view. Your dad thought I was crazy for bringing it along. Thought we'd be too busy to rifle through all his old stuff." She laughed. "He's probably right."

Ford reached for the briefcase. His head spun as his hand drew closer. He didn't care. He needed to open it.

"Uh-uh-uuuuuh," Mom said, gently nudging him towards the pile of suitcases. "Later, ma' boyo."

The moment Mom disappeared out the apartment doorway, Ford wrapped his fingers around the handle of Great-Granddad's briefcase. His vision blurred. He blinked and stumbled backwards. The hardwood floors paled, greying into concrete. The hallway walls wavered and flashed, just like when a storm messes with satellite television reception.

Goosebumps prickled up his arms. Was the apartment haunted?

Ford gripped the leather-covered handle of Great-Granddad's briefcase tighter, instinctively pulling it closer to his body. He blinked harder and when he opened his eyes, the walls around him slowly disappeared and in their place emerged an airport hangar. Where—how did he get here? He spun around, searching for his cousin. She was nowhere in sight. His heart raced.

"Ellie!"

The tang of diesel fuel filled his nostrils. A man in a uniform raced towards him yelling something in French and pointing to a single-engine prop plane—the kind you see in old black-and-white movies.

Then a bomb exploded and everything went black.

CHAPTER 5

"Ford!" Ellie's voice sounded muffled. "What are…"

Ford tried to listen, but he was too tired.

"Ford! Are you okay?"

Why was she yelling in his ear? Why wouldn't she let him sleep?

"Ford!"

Ford's eyes blinked open. Ellie's face was inches from his own. Her eyebrows scrunched tight.

His head pounded, his ears rang. "What happened?" Ford sat up and smashed his head. "Ow!" He looked up.

Why was he underneath the hall table?

"You went crazy. You grabbed the briefcase and then screamed 'look out' and dove under here. Why'd you do that?"

"I-I-I'm not sure…" Ford's words trailed away. A smell of sulfur and something else—concrete?— burned his nose. It began to run. He wiped it across his sleeve. What happened?

"Maybe I have jetlag."

"Jetlag? I don't think so. You looked terrified, like you saw a ghost."

"I-I," he stuttered, searching for words. Ellie's eyes bore into him, her frown etched deep across her forehead. He had no answers for her. His gaze locked onto the briefcase. It lay on its side down the hall, just outside the doorway to the living room where he had thrown it in his panic. The buckles had popped open and the contents were scattered across the floor. Ford shook his head. It throbbed harder and his vision began to swirl. He took a slow breath and closed his eyes.

When he opened them again, Ellie's face stared back, her eyebrows scrunched even tighter.

"You are holding out on me. Are you okay?" Ellie asked.

"I'm okay. I-uh…" Ford glanced at the briefcase. "It's going to sound insane."

Ellie kneeled next to him. Her hand on his shoulder. "Maybe, but you still have to tell me."

"I-I saw something or went somewhere or…I don't know. It was really…weird."

"That is weird and it doesn't make a lot of sense." She stared hard at him, as if she was trying to read his mind.

"I dunno. All I remember is seeing an airplane hangar and then, I think—uhm—a bomb exploded."

"A bomb exploded?" Ellie repeated. "Geez, I didn't know you had such a crazy imagination."

She leaped to her feet and sped to the case. Still too dizzy to stand, Ford crawled to where she hovered over a mess of postcards, letters, old pens, photos, and paper clips.

"All of this was in his bag?" he asked.

"Yeah. Who knew our genius great-grandfather was a hoarder of desk supplies?" She carefully picked up a ragged black-and-white photo of a restaurant.

Ford fought against his circling vision to stand beside her. "Let me see that." Ford reached for the picture. The moment his thumb and forefinger grasped it, the room spun. Scared, he dropped the photo and staggered away from Ellie.

"What's wrong? Ford!"

"Gotta…lie down." He leaned against the wall for support and shuffled towards his bedroom.

Ellie guided him through the doorway, shouldering his weight as he slumped against her. He flopped on the bed, moaning.

Ellie swung his legs onto the mattress. "I'm getting help. Don't move!"

Too tired to speak, his head sank deep into the soft pillow.

How could I go anywhere? I can't even see straight.

His eyelids were too heavy to lift, as if someone had placed tiny weights on them. The mere effort of thinking made his brain more sluggish.

So...strange...I...can't...

He sighed and that moment of relaxation was all his body needed. Within seconds he was asleep.

◆

He ran down a narrow alleyway. The walls of the buildings were so close he could almost touch each side if he stood still. But he couldn't stop. Someone was chasing him.

"Halt!" The man yelled, his German command echoing off the buildings.

Not likely. I must get past the checkpoint and to the safe house before dawn. Or I'm a goner.

He raced into the street, leaving the relative protection of the alley behind. There wasn't a soul on the road as he veered left, purposely heading away from his final destination.

I've come too far to let this Jerry get the upper hand.

Apartment buildings and storefronts flew by as he sped from the SS agent. He searched for the sign. A flash of light from a second-storey window at the far end of the street broke through the dark night. Another flash but this time longer, followed by a wink of light.

Thanks, Scout. Message received. I haven't much time. The officer chasing me will soon be joined by his chums and I can't outrun an entire troop.

He reached into the satchel that slapped his hip, finding what he needed. Without hesitation, he yanked the pin and swiveled around, hardly slowing, and threw the live grenade. He didn't wait to see it hit its mark. He ran faster, his legs burning and feet pounding on the pavement, his lungs screaming.

Must reach the next light post. That should be enough distance—

A blast of air hit him square in the back. Shrapnel pelted his calves. Pain shot up his legs. He flew forward, crashing to the cobblestone sidewalk, and rolled off the curb into the empty street, slamming into the tire of a parked car. He lay there, the wind knocked out of him, his head pounding. The only thing he could hear was his own heartbeat as it thumped loudly in his ears. He cradled his head in his hands, trying to focus his thoughts. He had to keep moving. His head snapped up.

The checkpoint.

CHAPTER 6

Ford sprang up, drenched in sweat. Bright sunlight trickled through the shutters and streamed across the floor. Groggy and confused, he stared around the empty room.

"Where am I?"

His throat burned as he tried to swallow. His leathery tongue slid across chapped lips. He flexed his feet. They felt sore, like he'd been standing for a long time—or running.

Running for his life? From Nazis?

He rubbed his calves. What would shrapnel feel like imbedded in his legs? He shook his head. It was only a dream. Ford sniffed and caught a faint whiff of something pungent—just like when he imagined that bomb explosion in the hallway. It sure had seemed real.

A glass of water sat on the bedside table. He took a gulp, untangled his legs from his blankets, and swung them over the side of his bed. Shivering, he grabbed his hoodie from the bedpost, slipped it on, and padded across the room. As he approached his closet, he noticed all his clothes hung in colour-coordinated rows. Ellie had been here.

Mom bustled into the room. She came to a dead stop. "What are you doing hiding in the closet?"

"I, ah—"

"Never mind. Get back to bed." She placed a tray of food on his bedside table. It was loaded with wedges of fresh breads, hunks of white and yellow cheeses, and a mound of fresh strawberries and raspberries. Ford's mouth watered as she plopped two large marshmallows into a mug of hot chocolate. He climbed under the sheets and she fluffed the bedspread over him.

"It took everything we had to keep your cousin out of your room. You were exhausted, kiddo."

Ellie bounded into the room and leaped onto his bed, swiping a large strawberry from his plate. "Finally! You missed an entire day, Monsieur Rip Van Winkle! You've been a total sad-sack for sixteen hours."

Aunt June followed Ellie into Ford's room. "Now, Ellie, sweetie, give Ford time to wake up."

Mom smiled at him. "Yes, you need to take it slowly. Bed rest for you today. You had us worried, young man. If it was up to me, I'd have you at the local hospital for a checkup, but your dad convinced me otherwise. Jetlag can be nasty. The adults are going on a walking tour of famous cemeteries, but you can get a hold of us on our cell phones. We'll only be gone a few hours. Now eat. You need something in your stomach." Mom linked arms with Aunt June. They bent their heads together and began discussing which famous person's grave they should see first.

Ellie watched them disappear down the hall.

"Hurry up. I've got something important to tell you and no way are we sticking around here all day." Her dark eyebrows arched high, vanishing under the rim of a Baltimore Orioles baseball cap. She leaned across Ford to snatch a raspberry from the plate then reared back, pinching her nose. "Peeuw. You reek! We do have time for you to shower." She howled with laughter.

Ford grabbed one of the throw pillows and chucked it at her head. She ducked and it sailed passed her into his father's face.

"Dad, I am so sorry."

"I guess someone's feeling better," he replied, smiling as he readjusted his glasses. He picked up the pillow and tossed it back on the bed. "Glad to see you back to your normal self."

"Yeah, I guess the flight knocked me out."

"Your first overseas trip is the trickiest. The more you travel, the better you get at it, and I agree with Ellie. Fresh air is just what you need." He patted Ford's shoulder and whispered. "I'll distract the moms while you three slip out."

"Wait. Us three?" Ford didn't even try to keep the whine from his voice. "Gavin is coming?"

"What did you expect? We'd let two thirteen-year-olds loose on the streets of Paris? You two are very mature, but even Ellie needs a chaperone sometimes."

"A chaperone! Come on Dad, it isn't 1920," Ford said.

"Listen, you're lucky I got your mother to agree to this. She wanted you to stay in bed for a good twenty-four hours. She may still change her mind, so unless you want to watch French soap operas all day, you had better get out that door."

"Fine." He crossed his arms. Gavin, just great.

"Thanks, Uncle Dave," Ellie added.

"Oh," Dad replied. "And one other thing I agree with Ellie about. You need a shower—extra soap." He winked at Ford, then left the room.

Ellie laughed so hard she nearly tumbled off the other side of the bed. Her cap flew to the floor.

"Hah! That'll show you!" Ford said, as he stuffed a huge hunk of soft white Brie cheese in his mouth. He'd never tasted anything so creamy.

"Chow down, Cuz. We've got some serious talking to do." Ellie pulled a photo from the front pocket of her hoodie.

Ford gasped. "The bug café?"

"The bug—wait. Did you think *magots* meant maggots, as in baby flies?" Ellie stopped talking. She had no choice. She was laughing too hard to speak.

Ford scowled at her. "Are you done yet?"

With her shirt sleeve, she dabbed tears from her eyes. "Sorry. Very loosely translated, *Les Deux Magots* means The Two Stocky Figurines from the East. Kind of a weird name, but it is definitely not The Two Bug Café."

"Good to know." Ford swallowed his embarrassment. He was too curious about the picture to get sidetracked. "Where did you get it?"

"That's what I need to talk to you about. This is the photo you were holding when you blacked out in the hallway and the photo has something to do with

Great-Granddad. I just overheard our parents talking about his mysterious war years and apparently the only thing he ever said about the war was that *Les Deux Magots* served the best *café au lait* in Paris."

"Huh."

"Yeah, and that's not all. Apparently, there is this big family rumour that Great-Granddad worked with a famous Canadian spy named William Stephenson and, to top it off, they found out a few months ago that Great-Granddad's nephew from Newfoundland was a codebreaker during the war at a place called Bletchley Park in England. He was trying to break secret German codes to win the war and your mom thinks Great-Granddad was up to some top-secret stuff too. Like James Bond 007 British spy work. Your mom got pretty excited at that prospect, but no one else did. It sounded like they didn't want to waste their time in Paris running around after hunches. Your dad kept telling her she was getting all excited over nothing and I agree. I mean, all we have are a bunch of old papers and photos."

"Maybe my mom's onto something. Before you came in here, I had this dream—" Ellie's scrunched-up face halted Ford's confession. She was too practical to think dreams meant anything in the light of day. "Never mind. Let me see the photo."

The moment his hand touched the picture, the room dimmed. His desk slowly faded.

"It's happening again," he mumbled.

Goosebumps raced across his arms as his desk completely disappeared, revealing a table and chairs.

His stark white bedroom wall shifted and trans-
formed into one that was butter yellow with white
trim. An ancient-looking wooden statue of an Asian
man quickly solidified, replacing the mirror that once
hung above his now-vanished desk.

He had to be hallucinating.

He blinked. The wooden statue remained.

Soft classical music and clinking silverware mixed
with voices, French voices. Beyond the table, he could
see shadows, but it was too hazy to make out details.

"Ellie?"

No response.

"Ellie do you see this?"

He scrunched his eyelids tightly closed. He must
be going crazy.

Please wake up!

Ford counted to three and opened his eyes. The fog
dissipated and an entire fancy restaurant emerged out
of it. A slender crystal vase holding a red rose sat at
every fine linen-draped table, and the men and women
who filled the restaurant didn't look like anyone he had
ever seen. At least not in real life. The women wore
either dresses or business suits with long skirts and all
wore a hat, tipped to the side. Many even wore elbow-
length gloves. Every single man had a dark suit and a
Fedora hat. Their ties looked super tight. Ford pulled
at the neck of his shirt. Not one pair of jeans in sight.
They looked like they walked off a 1940s Hollywood
movie set.

Ford's heart raced. Where was he?

"Ellie?" She was definitely not here.

A maître d' dressed in a long-tailed black tuxedo strode towards Ford. "*Monsieur, s'il vous plait suivez-moi.*"

Before Ford could answer, a gentleman next to him replied, "English, *s'il vous plait.*"

The maître d' sucked in a sharp breath and his mouth puckered as he glowered at the man. "Monsieur, please follow me," he said, in clipped, heavily accented English. His lips recoiled as if each word tasted bitter.

"*Merci,*" the man said as he tipped his grey hat. A small smile quivered at the edge of his mouth under his pencil-thin moustache. He smoothed down the white handkerchief that poked out of his lapel pocket.

This man seemed familiar somehow. Ford examined his short, sandy-blond hair and his grey-blue eyes, which were focused on a table across the room.

Maybe he could help me, tell me where I am.

"Sir, can you—" But the blue-eyed man was already across the restaurant, approaching a table occupied by three military officers. He saluted the officers and they raised their arms in response, red armbands flashed, angry black swastikas on display.

"Heil Hitler!" They chanted as one.

Ford staggered backward. Nazis? In Paris? Impossible. He spun around, nearly running into a waitress carrying a large tray of dirty dishes.

"Sorry," Ford said, but she didn't reply. She didn't even look at him. In fact, she didn't even slow down. Maybe she didn't understand English. "*Excusez-moi,*" he called after her in French. Still no reply. It was as if—

"Ford!" A girl's voice yelled. He fell backward. His head thunked against something hard. He blinked. Invisible hands gripped his shoulders and shook him. The restaurant faded away and his Paris bedroom reappeared. Cold water splashed across his face.

Ford bolted upright, sputtering, and wiped water from his face with his shirt sleeve. Ellie stood over him, an empty water glass in her hand.

What...what just happened?

CHAPTER 7

Ford finally managed to speak. "Why did you throw water on me?"

"I didn't have a choice. I couldn't wake you up. You were in some sort of freaky trance. What happened to you?"

"I'm not sure." The picture of the restaurant lay in his lap. He must have dropped it when Ellie shook him. A shiver ran down his neck and it wasn't from the cold water. "I was sitting here, holding the photo and then presto, everything went blurry and the room...changed."

"Changed?"

"Yeah, everything morphed into a restaurant." Ford's hand shook as he pointed to the photo. "I think it was that restaurant—*Les Deux Magots.*" Definitely not a bug café.

Ellie picked up the picture. "Your bedroom morphed into...this restaurant?"

"Yes. It was like I was there. I could see and hear everything, but—"

"Are you saying you magically shrank into this photo?" Her brow furrowed.

"No. I mean...I don't think so...I didn't shrink, exactly..." Was he somehow being transported into a different time and place, through old photographs, like some kind of modern-day Alice in Wonderland? That just didn't feel right. "If I actually shrank, you would've seen it."

"Right, so what happened?"

"It's hard to explain. It's sort of a feeling of…" he struggled to find the right words. "…of déjà vu, as if I've seen everything before and I'm just reliving it, or remembering it. But at the same time, I felt like I was really there in that restaurant surrounded by real people, but I couldn't have been…"

"Well, obviously you weren't really there because you were right here on your bed and I was standing right next to you, watching you stare into the great beyond."

"No, that's not what I meant. When I touched the picture and I went wherever I went, I tried to talk to a waitress and she couldn't hear me."

"Actually, you did mutter a whole bunch."

"Really? What did I say?"

"I dunno, just some mumbo jumbo—French mumbo jumbo. And you mumbled my name a few times. Maybe you were having some sort of awake dream?"

Ford shook his head. "That doesn't seem right either." All the blood rushed from his face. "Everyone in that restaurant spoke French and there was this one man who looked like I should know him. I felt like I'd seen him before…or something. And then he…he sat down with Nazis. And it felt so real. They felt so real." He clenched his comforter. "What do you think is happening to me?"

Ellie didn't reply, which was strange and made Ford nervous. Even if she didn't have an answer to something, she always had an opinion. A loud opinion. But this time she was too quiet.

Ford's booming heartbeat filled the silence.

Dad poked his head back into the room. Both Ellie and Ford jumped.

Ford hoped he appeared calm. "Hey...Dad."

"Why haven't you showered yet? I can't hold off a pair of worrying moms for much longer. And kids, I need you to go easy on Gavin. He's had a rough year, which is why he's with us this summer. He's had a tough time."

Gavin's had a tough time? What would Dad say if he knew Ford just had a Nazi hallucination? "He's had a rough year?" Ford asked, wondering what rough would look like to a brilliant math prodigy. Ford struggled to get Bs, even in Phys. Ed.

Dad peered over his glasses at Ford. "Just be nice, okay?"

"Okay," Ford and Ellie said in unison, watching him disappear down the hallway.

"Pffff. What could Gavin be stressed about? He's got it made," Ford said, not adding that Ellie had it easy, too. Ford knew he sounded bitter, but it sucked that he was the only one who hadn't inherited the genius genes.

"I think it would be pretty nerve-wracking going to university in another province when you're only sixteen. He left everyone he ever knew behind and it's not like he's the most outgoing guy. Didn't Gavin get too homesick to go to sleepaway camp?"

"Yeah. My parents had to drive out to Camp Augusta to pick him up after three nights when he was fourteen." Maybe Gavin wasn't having the time of his life after all. He swallowed a nauseating lump that rose in his throat. Maybe he'd been too hard on his brother. "I wasn't exactly happy he was coming to Paris. Do you think he could tell?"

"Ah, yeah. You have perfected 'jealous brother' face. At least now you can make it up to him."

"Yeah, I guess so."

"Anyway, we have to hurry. I'll go grab my backpack. I've got all of Great-Granddad's old photos in there, my phone, and—"

"Ellie," Ford interrupted her. "You never said what you thought was happening to me."

"We'll figure it out." She flashed her normal, confident smile that made her eyes twinkle. "But first, you need to rid yourself of that nasty B.O."

"Ok, ok." He popped a strawberry in his mouth and climbed out of bed.

She flew to his doorway and then stopped dead. "And one more thing. We have to tell Gavin."

"No way. He's never going to believe me. What if he tells Mom and Dad and they think I am completely nuts? What if he teases me for the rest of my life? What if—"

Ellie faced him, hands on her hips. "No more what ifs. He is your brother, he will believe you *and* he is insanely smart *and* it will help you make amends for being such a crummy brother."

"But—"

Ellie shushed him with her finger. "Plus, you promised your dad you would be extra nice."

Ford shrugged. The last person he wanted to know about these weird visions was Gavin, but it was no use arguing with Ellie. "Fine."

"Do you or do you not want to find out why you keep spacing out on me?"

"Of course." Not only was he curious, he was totally freaked out. Yet these hallucinations—or whatever—they sort of thrilled him and that freaked him out even more. How was it possible for one person to feel so many conflicting emotions at the same time?

Ellie eyed him. Her eyebrows creased like they always did when she was deep in thought. "You're scared," she declared.

"Uhm—"

She stepped closer, pulling off her cap. Her loose hair fuzzed around her head like a halo. She stood with her nose millimetres from his and stared directly into his eyes. "Me too," she admitted, her eyebrows relaxing into their normal position. A huge smile took over her face, her eyes alight. "Don't you just love that feeling?"

"Ah, not really."

She laughed. "Poor you! Now get ready!"

Ellie skipped out of the room, leaving Ford alone with his thoughts and the photo of the *Les Deux Magots* on his pillow. He leaned over his bed, examining the restaurant in the picture. His hands balled into fists, hiding his fingers so they wouldn't strike out and grab it. Intuition told him that if he was going to have another episode, Ellie should be nearby.

Intuition also told him it wasn't a matter of if he had another episode, but when.

This time Ford planned to be ready.

CHAPTER 8

"So what do you think?" Ford asked Gavin.

Ford had expected his brother to laugh and tell him he was stupid, well maybe not stupid exactly. Gavin was never really mean, but he had a way of talking that confused Ford and made him feel stupid. Now Ford was confused again by Gavin, but it wasn't because of what he said. This time it was his brother's silence. Gavin hadn't uttered a word since they sat down in the coffee shop. He just sat there, stone-cold quiet, while Ford told him about his hallucinations or episodes or—whatever they were. The only sound Gavin made was slurping his cappuccino.

"I'm not sure what to think. I wonder…" Gavin's words trailed off. He folded his napkin over and over into a tiny square. Ford's hands began to sweat as he waited impatiently for Gavin to continue. His brother unfolded the napkin to its original size and pointed to it. "Isn't that interesting? Depending on how you look at something, your perception of it changes. Is this a large napkin or a small square? The answer? Both."

Ford shook his head, puzzled. "What has that got to do with these episodes I keep having?" This was the kind of talk that Ford hated.

"Maybe nothing, but the most difficult math problems have often been solved by looking at them in a different way."

"What the heck does math have to do with me?" Math, the foreign language that left Ford confused for days.

"Not math directly, but there is a philosophical quest—" Gavin stopped talking as Ford sighed and rolled his eyes. "Right, not interested in philosophy. Did you tell Mom and Dad about this?"

Ford scoffed. "Of course not. Mom would have stuck me on permanent bed rest and Dad would have gone along with her."

Gavin nodded. "True."

Ford was afraid to ask Gavin the next question. "What I really want to know is, do you think I am going crazy?"

"Crazy? No way. There has to be an explanation. We just need to look at this from a different angle, an angle that may not be obvious. We'll find you some answers."

Ellie bounded towards them with a bag of fresh croissants. "Sustenance," she said as she plunked her backpack on the table. Hot chocolate sloshed over the rim of Ford's mug.

"Gavin thinks we'll find some answers," Ford said.

"See! I knew you'd be an asset!" Ellie said to Gavin. "Ford wasn't so sure."

"What? I-I," Ford stuttered, glaring at Ellie.

"Don't worry about it. I know we don't always get along. Sometimes I can be a know-it-all. At least that's what I've been told," Gavin said, blushing.

"Hah! Me too! But how is it our fault that we know so much?" Ellie laughed and passed the *Les Deux Magots* postcard to Gavin. "This is the photo Ford touched back at the apartment. This is the restaurant he zoned out to or into or—whatever you want to call it."

Gavin flipped it over in his hands, then looked at Ellie. "Nothing happens when you or I touch it, so it must be Ford specific." He shifted his attention to Ford. "Did anything really stand out for you when you had this...vision?"

Ford nodded. "Yeah, there was this man, he was around the same age as Dad, with short, sandy-blond hair, a moustache, and grey-blue eyes. I felt like I knew the guy—like I'd met him before." Ford looked down at the table as fear rolled up from his belly. "And there were Nazi officers with him."

"Nazi officers? Like during World War 2?"

"I guess."

"Hmmm. And you said you felt like you'd met this man before? Huh. It does sound impossible, except... Ellie, can I see the stuff from the briefcase?" Gavin asked.

"Sure." Ellie withdrew a bundle of photos, post-cards, and letters from her backpack.

Gavin leafed through them. "Aha. These ones will do." He pulled three black-and-white photos from the pile and held them in front of Ford. Two pictures were of dark-haired German officers and one was of a civilian in a dark suit with lighter hair. "Does the man from your vision look like any of these men?"

"That one." Ford pointed at the photo of the man in the suit. "Who is it?"

"That, little brother, is our great-grandfather, so in a way you do know him. At least through family stories and old photos." Gavin flipped it over. "Someone's written 'Paris, 1944' here."

Ellie sat back in her chair. "So, you think Ford is connecting with our long-dead great-grandfather? That is too weird to be true."

"Actually, it's not entirely weird. Ford is simply experiencing something that is unexplainable, at least unexplainable to us. In science, we seek answers to the unexplainable all the time and, like scientists, we need to think outside the norm if we are going to work this out." Gavin tapped the handle of his cappuccino mug with his thumb. "I have an idea and I need you to keep an open mind…"

"O-kay…" Ford replied slowly. He tensed at his brother's hesitation.

"Good. Now, you may think I am going to the extreme and it's going to sound bizarre coming from me, but I really think we need to research psychic phenomenon."

"Psychic *what?*" Ford asked, his heart skipping a beat. His hands began shaking again. He pressed them to his thighs to steady his nerves. Or was he shaking more from excitement? Maybe Gavin was getting close to the truth.

"Psychic phenomena. Extra-sensory processing, known to most people as ESP, and there's telepathy, time travel, clairvoyance," Gavin said. "There are all sorts of different fields of study into the paranormal."

Ford laughed, which sounded hollow. "I thought you would have some sort of scientific answer."

"Science doesn't always give us easy answers. Sometimes we have to think creatively."

"How do you know so much about all this psychic stuff, anyway? I can't imagine they have an Introduction to the Paranormal class at McGill University."

"No, but I watch a lot of late-night documentaries while my roommates are out partying."

"Oh." Ford couldn't imagine a more lonely existence. No wonder Gavin came home for the summer.

"Paranormal. Hmmm. Interesting idea, unlikely but interesting," Ellie said, pulling her laptop from her bag. She placed it on the table and lifted the screen. It blipped to life within seconds. "Clairvoyance. Why didn't I think of that?"

"Maybe because you're the kind of person that has to see it to believe it and maybe you don't have all the answers to everything," Ford said.

Ellie punched him in the arm. "Funny." She began typing and within seconds an entire list of entries popped onto the screen. Ford watched Ellie run her finger down the left side of the monitor reading Google results out loud. "*Clairvoyance—witchy woman*; *Clairvoyance—The Board Game*; *Clairvoyance— How to Predict Lotto Numbers*; *Clairvoyance by Chloe—First 10 Minutes Free*. That's it! Chloe the clairvoyant. She sounds like a winner!"

"No way. Keep going."

Ellie scrolled to the bottom of the screen.

"How about..." Ford said as Ellie scrolled through entry after entry. "This one. *Clairvoyance—A Gentle Beginning—Madame Bellerose*—Appointments Available—379 Rue D'Hugot, Paris. This one looks good."

Ellie typed the address into her phone. "It's too far to walk, so we'll have to catch a bus."

Ford clicked on the entry. An enormous, black, wrought-iron clock filled the screen.

"What is that?" Ellie asked. "It's crazy. It has... sixteen hands! It must be some sort of modern art creation from some wacko artist. This is a dead end."

Ford scanned the clock face. He was sure he'd never seen it before, but it seemed right to him. The clock dissolved and the screen darkened to a charcoal grey. Four pencil-thin black words slowly appeared.

Time. Is. Not. Linear.

Gavin leaned in close, then looked up at Ford and Ellie. "This is not a dead end. This may be the beginning."

"Time is not linear. What does that even mean?" asked Ford.

Ellie sipped her hot chocolate. "Maybe you've uncovered yet another mystery."

"Or uncovered some answers," said Gavin. "It's funny, Einstein believed in timelessness. He believed that the past, present, and future all happen simultaneously. It is all part of his Theory of Relativity. But then, and this is where things get really interesting—this other physicist, Richard Feynman, developed his own theory called Sum over Histories, which led him to describe time simply as a direction in space."

"My dad gave me Feynman's book to read this summer! So far *Sum over Histories* is really cool." Ellie said, her smile engulfing her face.

"For sure. You'll love it. And of course, there's Stephen Hawking, who in my humble opinion is tied with Einstein as the most influential physicist of all time, no pun intended. He has an even more exciting theory called Imaginary Time, meaning—"

"Stop!" Ford said.

"What's wrong?"

"Gavin, you lost me at timelessness, and Ellie, I cannot get past the image of you reading about science theory on your summer holiday."

Ellie laughed. "Sorry, Cuz."

Ford laughed with her. "Can you just give me a quick summary?"

Gavin nodded. "I'll try. What all those physicists are suggesting is that we don't really understand how time works and, in fact, many different universes or realities of our world could be happening at the same time. It also could mean the past, present, and future are all happening right this very moment, not just in a straight line forward."

"Sounds like a sci-fi novel," Ford said.

Gavin thumped Ford on the back. "It is exactly like a sci-fi novel."

A warmth spread through Ford. For once he understood something scientific that came out of Gavin's mouth. "Huh. Maybe what's happening to me is that somehow I am tapping into the past while being here in the present and, for whatever reason, I am connecting with Great-Granddad."

Ellie shook her head. "I don't know about that. That's a huge leap. You have to remember these are just theories."

"No, Ellie. I think Ford may be onto something."

She stared at Gavin as if he had a third eye. "You can't be serious."

Gavin smiled at Ford. "100 percent serious. Scientists must keep their minds open to all possibilities. That's how some of the greatest thinkers have made the most important scientific discoveries. It takes a dreamer to come up with an idea or concept that no one else has even considered."

Ford grinned and returned to reading the clairvoyance webpage. "We can make an appointment online." He clicked on the website's calendar and typed in his name and email address "We're in for eleven o'clock."

Ellie leaped to her feet. "Okay, let's go. I've got the psychic's address mapped in my phone."

Gavin and Ford clambered after her as she raced out the shop and down the street. She held her phone out in front of her, the GPS guiding her steps.

"Hurry, ma' boyos!" she trilled in a perfect imitation of Ford's mom.

Ford shook his head. "She has got to stop that. One yodeler in the family is more than enough."

CHAPTER 9

They piled onto the bus, taking seats in the first row. Ford's hands were sweaty, and not just from running on a warm summer day. Normally he'd play a game on his phone, but the past twenty-four hours had been so unbelievable, he just needed to think. He closed his eyes and let his head fall back against the seat.

What would the psychic tell him?

Deep down, he knew he wasn't cracking up and knowing Gavin didn't think so either was more comforting than he expected, but these hallucinations were pretty freaky. And seeing Nazis? They terrified him more than anything. The strangest part of all was that each time he had a vision, he felt like he was actually there, wherever there was; everything looked so crisp and clear. Heck, he even smelled roasted garlic in that restaurant and he tasted dust in the air from that bomb explosion. How could that be possible? When he touched the briefcase and the photos, immediately a vision occurred, but then he had that dream and it was just as real as the visions and he hadn't touched anything. Frustration grew in the pit of his stomach. He hated not knowing what was happening. There had to be a pattern, but he couldn't see it.

"We're crossing the Seine," Ellie said, interrupting Ford's thoughts. "Not far now."

The bus meandered along, slowing and stopping, warm air flowing through the doors as people loaded and unloaded while Gavin and Ellie compared GPS apps. Ford pressed his nose to the window. Boats floated down the river below and tourists travelled in packs along the sunken walkway.

Gavin pointed out the window. "Look! The *Grand Palais!* Did you know they have a police station in the basement so they can secure the art exhibits at all times?"

Ford grinned at Gavin, who looked like going to an art gallery was as fun as seeing a hockey game was to Ford. "Maybe you should consider dumping quantum physics and become a tour guide, if you take a pass on history professor."

Gavin crossed his arms. "History is more of a hobby for me. I don't want to ruin it by turning it into my career."

"Right. History hobby. I think I'll stick with remote-control airplanes."

"Guys, we're almost there. We get off at the *rond-point des Champs-Elysées.*" Ellie shifted her backpack and stood as the bus slowed to a halt. They climbed off, following Ellie and the GPS instructions on her phone. "This way." She led them across the roundabout and past mansion after mansion. They took a quick left, then darted down an alley before arriving at an older and far narrower cobblestoned street. She looked up from her mobile at the boys. "Getting closer."

The apartment buildings seemed ancient to Ford. Low, metal fences encased small front gardens.

"This is it," Ellie announced.

"Are you sure we're at the right place?" Gavin asked.

Dark green vines climbed up the crumbling brick walls and across the windows on the first two floors. Chunks of the apartment's stone steps had fallen away and the rain gutters hung low, like a line of loosely strewn Christmas lights.

A nose-to-toe wave of déjà vu washed over Ford. Goosebumps erupted on his arms and blazed across his body. He grabbed the wrought-iron fence to steady himself. Something—or someone—was pulling at him, calling him towards the building. "This is definitely the right place. I can feel it in my bones." Ford's voice sounded distant to his own ears.

Ellie smiled. "That may be the single spookiest thing you have ever said." She pushed at the black gate. It screeched open, scraping across the cobblestones. She dusted her fingers on her jeans and marched toward the front door.

A shiver ran from the nape of Ford's neck, over his shoulders, and rippled out across his back. "Hopefully Madame Bellerose isn't as scary as this building is," he mumbled.

"I'm sure she's fine, I'm sure she's a sweet psychic," Ellie said as she climbed the stairs and stopped in front of an old intercom panel. "Suite 379." She punched in the apartment number.

"*Monsieur* Crawford MacKenzie?" a voice crackled from the speaker in the wall.

Ford slipped past Ellie to stand directly in front of the intercom. "Yes, that's me. It's Ford."

"*Bonjour* Ford. Please, if you will, close the gate and then *entrez-vous, s'il vous plait.*"

"Ok—*oui,*" said Ford. How did she know the gate was left open? He pushed it shut and followed Ellie and Gavin into the dim entranceway.

"Third floor. There won't be an elevator in this place," said Gavin.

Ford stared up the staircase. A mahogany banister, missing a spindle—or three—banked the stairs. An earthy, musty smell filled Ford's lungs. He coughed.

Ellie stepped on the first stair. A loud creak filled the foyer. "This building is a bit of a wreck."

Ford whistled. "It was probably incredible back in the dark ages when it was built."

"That is a bit of an exaggeration. The style of architecture dates from the mid to late 1700s," said Gavin.

"Exactly what I was thinking! You can tell by the fine detail—" began Ellie as they climbed the stairs.

Ellie and Gavin nattered on about every last inch of the building, suggesting various architects as the possible designer as Ford followed them up the winding staircase. He tried to tune them out, but he couldn't completely block their conversation. His irritation with their endless knowledge of every single thing grew with each squeaky footstep. When they got to the third floor, he couldn't take it anymore.

"All right, all right, I get it. You guys know everything about everything!"

"What—what do you mean?" Ellie said, taking a few steps down the hallway.

"Physics, historical figures, Paris, and even architecture?! You two may know everything, but you know nothing about this." Ford tapped his temple with his index finger. "Even Gavin the Perfect said so. Whatever is going on in here, you have no clue about it. Nada. Nil. Nothing."

"I never said I was perfect," Gavin said.

"And I—" Ellie sputtered.

"And the thing is, this isn't about you. Neither of you. It's about me..." Ford said and then muttered, "for once."

Gavin's face flushed. "O-kay, I'm not sure why you are suddenly so angry."

"Because everything is always about you guys. Your grades, your hobbies, even how much better you speak French. Everything anyone in our family ever talks about is your massive brains and how much you are like our great-grandfather, 'the brilliant and can do no wrong' Edward Hugh Crawford!" Ford's anger lessened with every word he spoke. Now he simply felt scared and alone. "And maybe that is true, but I'm the one having this bizarre connection with him. I'm the one seeing into the past and it is totally freaking me out."

Ellie's jaw dropped.

Gavin stepped closer to Ford. "I am so sorry. I—"

A door opened behind them.

The oldest woman Ford had ever seen smiled and adjusted her glasses as her gaze slowly travelled over the cousins.

"*Excusez-moi, mes amis*, but you are disturbing the other residents. I am Mme. Bellerose."

CHAPTER 10

"Please, sit," Mme. Bellerose said, nodding at a loveseat that sat under a wide window. Sheer white curtains ruffled in the warm summer breeze.

Ford sat and Ellie plunked down so close to him, their elbows touched. Much to his surprise, he could feel her arm shaking. Knowing Ellie, it must be from excitement and not fear. The moisture in Ford's mouth dried and he cleared his throat. Gavin perched on the armrest on the other side of Ellie.

A blue, flowered teapot and four teacups sat on a simple dark wood table in front of them. Ford wasn't a huge tea drinker, but he'd drink an entire pot if it would stop his tongue from drying to jerky.

Mme. Bellerose slowly eased herself into a tall-backed, gold-brocaded armchair that sat opposite them. She rested her small hands on the chair's ornate arms, her fingers tracing the carved wood as she stared at Ford. Ford, trapped in her gaze, couldn't pull his eyes away from her. The little remaining moisture in his mouth evaporated as she silently interrogated him.

Could she read his thoughts?

His hands began to sweat. Why wasn't she saying anything? Wait, did she know he just thought that?

And what about now? And now…? Using all his effort, he broke her gaze and stared at the teapot. Maybe if he kept just thinking of nothing, she wouldn't be able to read his mind. But how do you think of noth—

"Hey, Ford!' Ellie shouted, pinching him on the thigh. "Mme. Bellerose just asked if you want some tea."

"Uhm, sorry, yeah, that would be great. Thanks," Ford replied, his dry mouth making his voice scratchy.

Mme. Bellerose smiled and lifted the tea strainer from the pot and rested it on the tray. "Most Parisians adore *café au lait*, but I've always been taken with tea. Would you care for lemon or sugar?" she asked as she poured him a cup.

"Both, I guess. Thanks."

She placed the teacup on the saucer and slid it across the tray towards Ford. She stared at the tea leaves as Ford grabbed the sugar bowl and plopped in two cubes and squeezed lemon into his cup. He stirred the tea quickly as a homey aroma filled his nostrils. Ford gulped. He finished it in seconds and placed the cup on the coffee table.

Mme. Bellerose smiled. "Better?"

Ford nodded.

"Let me look at you." She took one of Ford's hands. She examined the back of it, then flipped it over. "Ah, I see." She traced a line that ran from his wrist up between his thumb and pointer finger. Shivers rippled across his hand. "Hmmm. *Très bon*." She released him.

"What…what did you see?" Ford asked.

"So impatient. I am not done. Let me see you properly."

Her eyes widened for a moment as she reached across the coffee table and placed one hand on each side of his face. Surprised, he stiffened. Her palms were cool on his cheeks. "Ah, yes," she murmured before closing her eyes. Warmth rushed outward from her fingertips and across the back of his head, like a band of heat, relaxing him in the process.

Ford yawned, suddenly feeling exhausted. His eyelids grew heavy, but not as heavy as his head. It lolled to one side, then the other. He yawned once more, before fully relaxing.

Mme. Bellerose smiled and then released Ford. He blinked his eyes open, feeling drowsy.

"It is as I expected," Mme. Bellerose said. "You are a clairvoyant, as am I."

"A clairvoyant. Is that why I've been having these strange...episodes?"

"Yes, they are visions of the past. You will be a truly great clairvoyant one day."

Ford leaned forward, a wide smile on his face. "A genius clairvoyant?"

Mme. Bellerose laughed. She sounded like a young girl.

Ellie leaned forward. "A genius—" she began, but the old woman cut her off.

"Yes! Yes, Ford. I like that—a genius clairvoyant. But you are inexperienced. Your psychic ability is like a geyser exploding at will. In time, you will learn to guide your talent and train your mind to decipher the clues others left in the past, so you can solve their mysteries today. Their memories are like echoes lost in time. That is what you are tapping into: memories that are travelling through time, not bound by life or death. They will always be there, they just need someone like you who can hear them."

"Wow," Ford replied, a smile spreading across his face.

She smiled back.

"Wow indeed. But Ford, remember not everyone will be so willing to accept your gifts. You must guard this piece of you. Be very, very cautious with whom you share your abilities. From my experience, desperate people will stop at nothing to control a proven psychic, forcing them to use their gifts to perform cruel and vicious acts," she crossed herself. "I have known many who were turned into agents of evil. Ellie, Gavin, you may need to protect Ford."

Ford's smile disappeared.

Gavin looked from Mme. Bellerose to Ford. "Agent of evil? I don't like the sound of that."

As Ford sat up straighter, a small smile crept back onto his face. He couldn't help it. Agent of evil or not, he was a genius. He couldn't tell anyone, which was kind of a downer, but still it was the single most amazing thing that had ever happened to him.

And finally, he felt like he belonged in his family— his genius family.

"I don't know. This seems a little convenient," Ellie

said to Mme. Bellerose. "Why didn't we know Ford was a clairvoyant before now?"

Mme. Bellerose chuckled and poured herself another cup of tea. "Convenient? That is not how clairvoyance works. I believe Ford became aware of his ability for two reasons." She then spoke directly to Ford. "First, you tapped into your own great-grand-father's memories and he is a blood relative. Second, you are meant to do great things, solve mysteries locked in the past and help people. It is as if your gift grew tired of your ignorance of its existence and it pushed through hard so you could no longer ignore it."

Gavin frowned. "I'm still a little confused. Can my brother see anyone's memories? That seems pretty intrusive."

"No, it is not so simple. Ford must connect with that person in some way—through emotion, family relationships, or a personal belonging or artifact. There are many ways a connection can begin."

Ford let that sink in. It was a lot to accept.

Ellie's look of disbelief morphed into a huge smile. She leapt to her feet, her eyes sparkling. Ford knew that look of excitement. "Ford could solve every single mystery known to mankind! He could figure out if there really is a lost city of Atlantis, or what happened to the great Mayan civilizations, and if actual aliens live among us," Ellie said. "He could predict lottery numbers! We could be millionaires!"

Mme. Bellerose clapped her hands and laughed. "No, no, *ma chèrie*. That is not how it works either.

To begin with, Ford cannot see into the future, only the past."

Ellie's smile slid from her face. Her arms fell to her sides.

"So that means..." Ford said, tapping his thigh. "That as long as I have some sort of connection, I can see anyone's past memories?"

"Not exactly. Even with a connection, memories can remain untouchable and no one knows with complete certainty why that is. Many of us believe that some people's energies just won't allow it. What is important to remember is that even if there is a connection, the memories cannot be forced. Either they are accessible to you—the clairvoyant—or they are not. What we do know for sure is that a connection must come with a desire to know and to learn for both the sender and the receiver."

Ellie sighed and crossed her arms.

"I can imagine you are having trouble believing me," Mme. Bellerose said to her.

"Who wouldn't? It is pretty unbelievable: energies swirling around us, memories crying out to be heard, and Ford being part of some big community of psychics."

"In time, I hope you will come to believe in your cousin." Mme. Bellerose turned to Ford. "You must never use your gift to fulfill your own wishes. Use your gift to help others. That is where true happiness can be found and you will help right old wrongs and always, always trust your instincts. Your instincts will keep you on the correct path."

Ford shrunk into the couch. He liked being a psychic genius, but he wasn't sure he was up to the challenge Mme. Bellerose was giving him. "Help right old wrongs? You make me sound so important."

"Oh, you are, but so are Ellie and Gavin and your parents and the postman down the street. We all play our part. Each one of us. But some of us can have a greater impact. That is where the responsibility comes in. You must respect this part of yourself and use it wisely. You are a great psychic who can see into the past."

A cuckoo clock chimed, the small wooden bird popped out of its house marking the time.

Mme. Bellerose rose from her chair.

Ellie pulled Great-Granddad's papers and photos from her bag. "I know our time is up, but could you help us with these? We just need to know why they are significant."

Mme. Bellerose closed her eyes and held her hand out a few inches above the stack in Ellie's arms. She smiled and opened her eyes. "This is a puzzle you three must figure out."

"That's all you can tell us?" Ellie asked.

"I will tell you this: this is your destiny—to be here in Paris together, to journey through the past, and to right a wrong and through these old documents you will connect to your great-grandfather," Mme. Bellerose said as she walked down her hallway to the front door. Gavin and Ford followed close behind.

Ellie stuffed everything back into her bag and elbowed past the boys. "Our destiny? Journey through the past? Right what wrong? We need to know why and—"

"Now, I must say *au revoir*," Mme. Bellerose interrupted Ellie's protest. She clasped Ford's hand. "Remember, you will do great things." She then turned to Ellie and Gavin, Ford's hand remaining in her grip. "This puzzle cannot be solved with Ford's abilities alone. You two are essential. And remember, Ford may need your protection. *Adieu, mes enfants.* Good luck."

She gently nudged Ford through the doorway to join Ellie and Gavin.

"But, what—" Ford began.

"Ford, trust your instincts," she said and closed the door.

The click of the lock echoed in the empty corridor.

Gavin shuddered. "Well, that was…something."

Ellie stared at Ford. "Yeah, something. What do you think? Do you really believe her?"

Ford squared his shoulders. The old woman's words ran through his mind.

You are a psychic genius and you are going to do great things.

Trust your instincts.

His instincts told him to trust her. "Yes, I do."

Gavin smiled. "Me too. As unreal as it may sound, Ford being psychic makes the most logical sense."

"I am still not fully convinced, but if you two think so, we need to get busy," Ellie said with a sharp nod. "And I know exactly where we should begin." She typed madly on her phone. "A library. Time for some good old-fashioned research."

"Research?" Ford's heart sank. The last place he wanted to spend the rest of his first day—his first fully awake day in Paris, was a stuffy old library. "I thought we'd do something exciting."

"This will be exciting, Ford. It's just like Mme. Bellerose said, we are solving a puzzle and the puzzle is—" She paused for dramatic effect and looked up from her phone. She wiggled her dark eyebrows at Ford as she continued, "—our great-grandfather's shady past and why you are channelling his memories."

Ford couldn't stop from smiling. Everything was more fun with Ellie around, even if she had her doubts about him. He sighed. "Okay, okay. But a library? Really?"

"Yes, and we are not going to just any library. We're going to one that specializes in military history." She thumped him on the back. "We're talking about the Sainte-Geneviève Library."

"Right. Sounds great," he said, quickly trying to find a way out of her library adventure. "But don't we need to get back to the apartment before our parents do?"

"Their tour will take up the rest of the day and my dad said they won't be back until six o'clock. That gives us hours of solid research time." Ellie's eyes sparkled. Ford couldn't help but smile because who besides his cousin would get this excited over spending hours in a library?

"And if we run out of time, we can always go back to the library tomorrow," added Gavin.

Right. His brother.

CHAPTER 11

"Hours of research time. Sounds lame," Ford muttered as they traipsed down the stairs.

Ellie led the way out of Mme. Bellerose's apartment block and back to the bus stop. Two buses sat at the curb. Ellie pointed to the display screen above the front window of the second one. "That's the one we need."

They climbed aboard and swiped their travel pass cards through the reader. Every seat was taken, so they grabbed handrails. The bus pulled into traffic and Ford stared out the open window as Paris raced by. Distinct Parisian smells filled the bus: baked bread as they passed *la patisserie*, the pungent smell of coffee from a quaint corner *café*, and the strong perfume of *les fleurs* from a street-side florist all teased Ford's senses.

"We're actually in France," he said.

Ellie laughed. "Yes, my dear Watson. Thank you for finally noticing."

He leaned forward across the aisle, peering around other passengers so he could get a better look at the buildings. "Some of those must be really old—like centuries old and they're all so...French, aren't they?"

"Yeah, because we're in France. If it looked like Japan, we'd be in big trouble."

"Le hardee-har-har. You know what I mean."

Ellie laughed. "Yeah, I do."

Gavin poked his head between Ellie and Ford. "You know, Parisians are lucky. I read the Germans never ransacked the city like they did everywhere else because even Nazis knew great architecture and works of art when they saw it."

Gavin and Ellie began a deep discussion about World War 2, which Ford knew nothing about. He watched his brother's face light up as he recited by heart the key dates of each major battle. Ford shook his head. Could they be any more opposite? He never would have thought to compare a math problem to solving the mystery of his visions. What had Gavin said? They needed to look at the problem differently? And he had been right. Of course.

Ford glanced at Gavin and pushed down a rising surge of jealousy. It had never seemed fair that both Ellie and Gavin were Einstein-smart like their great-grandfather, but today all that changed. Now he was in the Genius Club, too. He wanted to shout it out loud, but since he had to keep his abilities a secret, that wasn't possible. He'd have to settle for convincing Ellie of it.

The bus squealed to a halt and the passengers leaned forward and rocked back, moving as one. Ellie stood on tiptoes and peered out the front window. "This is our stop." She moved to the exit.

The trio stepped onto the sidewalk, and as the bus pulled away, Ford's mouth fell open. Across the road stood an enormous building that looked like it belonged more in Rome than France. Six stone pillars rising thirty feet high supported a huge triangular pediment and carved into it was a scene of a woman passing out crowns. At least a dozen more columns towered behind that one, supporting a massive dome.

"Wow! I never knew a library could look so amazing!" Ford said.

"It is impressive, but the outside is nothing compared to the inside," Ellie replied.

"It must be incredible."

"Wait! Ford." Ellie tugged at his arm. "You are looking at the wrong building." She turned him completely around and pointed to a building that stood behind him. "This is *La Bibliothèque Sainte-Geneviève*. The building you were looking at is the Pantheon."

"Oh." Ford's heart sank, draining his enthusiasm as his excitement plummeted deep into his chest. The library was a boring, large, rectangle-shaped building. It would've fit right into the Old Market Square area of Winnipeg. He glanced back at the Pantheon. Goosebumps rose along his arms.

"Ellie, there's something about that building—I have that déjà vu feeling."

"Hmmm..." she replied, patting her backpack. "There was a photo of the Pantheon in the briefcase and also a letter that mentions it."

"Do you think that means the Pantheon was important to Great-Granddad?" Ford asked.

"I don't know. You're the one who will know for sure, at least according to the all-knowing Mme. Bellerose."

Ford decided to ignore her jibe. "Maybe I should hold one of the photos and see if I can tap into a vision."

"Woah, woah, woah," Gavin said, shifting his bag from one shoulder to the other. "Guys, before we start following Great-Granddad's memories all over Paris, we need to know as much as possible about him so we aren't jumping into this blindly. If Ford is going to go wandering into our great-grandfather's past, we should be better prepared."

"Good point. Research calls and that I can get excited about," said Ellie. "C'mon Ford."

Ford slowly tore his eyes from the Pantheon and together the cousins sprinted across the parking lot to the library's arched doorway. Ellie led them up the stairs, and they slowed as they entered the building, their footfalls echoing through the entranceway and up the two-storey-high arched ceilings.

"Let's go..." Ellie looked into the library proper. "This way." She led them into a room as long as a football field, its high, arched ceiling just like the cathedrals Mom had shown him in preparation for this trip. The carved wood and ornate decorations were far more impressive in real life.

"Wow, I've never been in a building with forty-foot ceilings before. This totally reminds me of the dining hall at Hogwarts," Ford said, staring around the cavernous room.

"It is awe-inspiring, isn't it?" Gavin said.

"Yeah, awe-inspiring," Ford repeated. Why couldn't his brother speak like every other normal sixteen-year-old on the planet? It was like living with a sixty-year-old grandpa. An extremely bright sixty-year-old grandpa who preferred solving math problems to playing video games.

They followed Ellie past row after row of long wooden tables that ran the width of the library. Each table had four lamps on it and each lamp had a glass shade the exact colour of a Granny Smith apple. Ford rubbed his stomach. He shouldn't have let Ellie rush him through breakfast.

Hopefully she thought to schedule a lunch break into their first "fun-filled" Paris day.

CHAPTER 12

"Take a deep breath, boys," Ellie instructed as they reached the library's information desk.

Ford stared at her, puzzled. "Why?"

"Just do it."

Ford and Gavin inhaled.

"Don't you just love that smell?" Ellie's grin was huge, her brown eyes bright. Ford shook his head. Maybe she was the one losing her mind. He took another deep whiff.

"Sure. It's very"—he paused, searching for the right word—"library-esque."

Ellie rolled her eyes. "It's the smell of parchment, ancient books, and history," Ellie's voice grew in volume, "and culture and knowledge and—"

"I wish it was the smell of a burger and fries," Ford interrupted. "I'm starving."

"You are a Neanderthal," she proclaimed and pinched him in the arm. Gavin stifled a laugh and stepped behind Ford, well out of Ellie's reach. Ellie slung her bag onto the dark mahogany counter. The metal clasps on her backpack clanked on the wood.

"*Excuse-moi,*" an older man called to Ellie. He sprung from a tall-backed leather chair, pointing at her backpack. "*Ce n'est pas une cafétéria. Retire ton sac.*"

Ford couldn't follow anything he said, but there was no misunderstanding his curt tone. The librarian glared at Ellie as she carefully removed her bag.

"*Je suis désolée,*" Ellie apologized, her face flushed red.

"Ah," he said, scoffing. "American." He spat out the word.

"What did she do wrong? He spoke too fast for me to follow," Ford whispered to Gavin.

Gavin nodded to the counter. "Apparently it is very rude to place your bag there."

"How may I help you?" the librarian asked, his gaze travelling from Ellie to Ford and finally to Gavin, his lips pressed into a tight line. His nose twitched, as if he smelled something foul.

"Looks like he thinks we're garbage and the only place he wants to help us is out of the building to the trash can," Ford whispered to Ellie.

"Shhh," she said to him and then smiled at the librarian. "We're looking for information about World War 2."

"Can you possibly narrow down the search? As you see, the war raged on long before you Americans got involved."

"Maybe this will help." Ellie pulled out a handful of old photos and pointed to the counter. "I can place *these* here, right?"

Ford cringed at the sarcasm in her voice. Dad needed to talk to her about getting more bees with honey than vinegar.

"Of course," the man replied. An equal amount of irritation laced his words. Ellie had met her match. The librarian glanced at his watch. "*Je m'excuse*. It is now time for my lunch. *Au revoir*." He nodded to them, picked up his briefcase, and draped his blazer over his shoulder.

"But," Ellie said, as he brushed past them. He didn't say another word before vanishing through a door that was almost completely hidden in the wood-panelled walls.

"Where did he go?" Ford asked.

"To lunch, I guess," Gavin said.

Ellie looked around the room. "I suppose we can just look through the stacks ourselves…"

Ford's jaw dropped as he followed her gaze. Banking the walls of the entire second floor were books. They ran the entire length of the long, rectangular library. "No way! There's got to be hundreds, no, thousands of books up there, and what if they are all in French?"

Ellie tilted her head to the side, examining the shelves. "There has to be a way." She pursed her lips. "Hmmm." Ford knew she was deep in planning mode.

"*Excusez-moi. Avez-vous été servis?*" a woman asked from behind Ford, tapping him on the shoulder.

"Have we been served?" Ford repeated her question in English as he turned to face her. His face grew slack, his eyes softened. "No, not really. I-I mean, *non*."

"Oh, Americans!" the French woman said, clapping her hands. She pushed a lock of long, honey-blonde hair behind her ear. Her blue eyes shone behind her stylish black-rimmed glasses. "Please, let me speak to you *en anglais*—I should say, in English. I need much practising."

"I'm Canadian actually and you can practise on me," Ford replied.

"Or me," Gavin offered, shouldering Ford out of the way. "I'm Canadian too."

"Oh, brother." Ellie rolled her eyes at them both.

The young librarian smiled at Ellie and asked, "Are they your...brothers? Are you..." she paused for a moment. "Siblings? Is that the right word?"

No one ever guessed that Ellie was their sister, which was fairly reasonable thanks to Ford and Gavin's vampire-pale skin and Ellie's darker, mellow-bronze complexion. In fact, some people didn't even believe they could be cousins. According to Ellie, those people were unevolved cretins.

"Yes, siblings is correct, but they're both my cousins."

"Ah, yes." The librarian glanced between the boys and Ellie. "I can see you and the younger one have matching freckles."

"Yes, that is one of the few things Ford and I have in common. My cousins, though, are both numbskulls," Ellie said.

"Numb-skulls?" She repeated, her shiny, pink, lip-glossed mouth forming each syllable. Ford's heart-beat cantered in his chest. He'd never met a girl like her. She was prettier than any girl he had ever seen.

"It means they are being idiots." Ellie elbowed Ford hard in the ribs. He stumbled into Gavin, who slammed into the high counter.

"Ford!" Gavin said between gritted teeth as he pushed Ford back.

"It wasn't me!" Ford shoved Gavin.

"Ah," the woman said. "You act like siblings, like my brother, Jean-Paul and I. We tease and fight, but we are best friends too."

Ford glared at Ellie. "I bet you don't call Jean-Paul a numbskull."

The woman chuckled. "No, he is my little brother so I call him *mon petit andouille*. It is like saying...my little goof. So it is almost the same, yes?"

"Sort of. I bet you're the nicest sister in the world. I bet you're never bossy," Ford said, still scowling at Ellie.

Ellie spoke through a forced smile. "Knock it off, Ford. We're here to get help."

"That is correct. How can I help you, Ellie and..." the librarian looked at the boys. She pulled at her ear, frowning. She said something so quietly Ford couldn't understand it. She then shrugged her shoulders and continued. "How can I help you, Ellie and...Fork? Your name is Fork? Is that correct?" she asked. "Your name is like, *argenterie*...silverware?"

Ellie squealed with laughter. Gavin joined in.

Ford didn't utter a sound. He couldn't. He was too busy dying of embarrassment.

"This is too good." Ellie gasped for breath. "I think I'll call you Fork, no, The Forkster from now on!"

Ford's whole body burned. Pretty soon he'd burst into flames if Ellie didn't shut up.

The librarian looked from Ellie to Ford. "Did I say something funny?"

"No, it's just—my name is Ford. F-O-R-D," he said, ignoring Ellie's giggles. "We're trying to find out what our great-grandfather did in World War 2. It is a big family mystery. We have some photos and letters and we want to piece it together."

"Ah, yes, that is a fascinating time period. I am the right *bibliothécaire* to assist you. And Ford," she said his name carefully, while squeezing his hand. "You must call me Marie-Claire."

Ellie squeezed his other hand, then spoke to Ford in a slow, kindergarten-teacher voice. "*Bibliothécaire* means librarian."

"I know what it means." He would've punched Ellie, but he was too focused on the invisible imprint Marie-Claire's fingers left on his hand to clobber his cousin.

"And I'm Gavin, *Fork's* older brother."

"Gavin!" It took every last ounce of restraint Ford had not to jump on Gavin's back and give him a life-changing nuggie.

Marie-Claire nodded and smiled at Ford. "What is the other reason you are here?"

"I need information about, about—" Ford began, but Marie-Claire licked her glistening lower lip and all thought in Ford's brain froze.

"Are you okay? Are you having another vision?" Ellie asked.

Gavin glared at Ellie.

"You have...visions?" Marie-Claire asked. She frowned.

Ford's face flushed, heat seared across his cheeks and up his ears. He took a big gulp, hoping she didn't think he was a lunatic. "Ah—yeah, sort of, but not right now. Just—never mind…" Ford's words dried in his mouth.

Marie-Claire's eyebrows furrowed for a moment and then relaxed as her mouth slid into a smile. She looked over the counter, scanning the long room. She gave a quick nod of her head. "Come with me." She led them around the counter to the librarian's desk and sat down at the computer. "Let us begin the search for the war history, *oui?*"

"*Oui*," Ford repeated.

Ellie shook her head. "You are pitiful."

Gavin shouldered in front of Ford. "Never mind. Let's get to work while Ford's still capable of simple sentences."

"Come along, *mes amis*, let us discover the secrets lost in the past," said Marie-Claire, ending their argument.

Ellie whooped loudly, then covered her mouth. "Sorry, just excited that you're talking *my* language. Can you please do a search for Edward Hugh Crawford?"

"*Oui*," Marie-Claire's perfectly manicured, shimmering silver fingernails flew across the keyboard.

"*Oui*," Ford whispered, as he stood behind her chair. A soft lavender scent wafted up his nose. He sighed.

Ellie rolled her eyes. "*Oui, oui, oui.* Ford, you are a ginormous *andouille!*"

Ford's hands balled into fists as he glared at Ellie. "Well you are an irritating know-it-all!"

"No fighting, *mes amis*." Marie-Claire winked at Ellie. "Your cousin, he is sweet, *non?*"

Ford smiled, his eyes went soft. "She called me sweet."

Ellie laughed. "Geez, *Fork*. She meant you're sweet like a lost Dalmatian, not like she wants to marry you. You better take a few deep breaths before you faint."

"Hey—" Ford began, but Marie-Claire cut him off.

"Let us get to work." Her voice was firm, with a large dose of big-sister authority.

"*Oui,*" said Ford and Gavin in unison.

"Oh barf," said Ellie, as shook her head at her cousins. "*Très, très* barf."

CHAPTER 13

Gavin frowned and crossed his arms. "Marie-Claire, why can't we find any information about our great-grandfather's war years on the internet?"

"It is very strange," Marie-Claire agreed. "We can find his old school records, when he was accepted into Oxford as a Rhodes Scholar, and then nothing. It is like someone has taken a giant eraser and removed all traces of his life between 1939 and 1947. Then *voilà,* in 1948 we find information about him."

Ellie sighed and closed a three-inch-thick text and placed it on the top of a tower of leather-bound books stacked high on the counter next to Gavin. "And it's great that we have all these history books, but there's almost too much information. I mean, we've been at this for an hour and a half and are we any further ahead?"

"At least you and Gavin are good at reading French. If it was left to me, we'd be here for the rest of our lives."

Ellie sat on the floor next to Marie-Claire's desk and opened her bag. "True. There has to be a clue somewhere in all his documents." She pulled out the letters, postcards, and photographs, along with every other "just in case of emergency item" she packed.

Out tumbled a stapler, scissors, two notepads, a small baggie of different-sized Band-Aids, and numerous pens and pencils. Ford stifled a giggle. There was even a pair of plastic vampire teeth. Did she think they might go to a costume party while on vacation? No one could ever accuse her of being unprepared. She would make the best Boy Scout. Ellie pushed her emergency supplies back into her bag and spread the papers in a circle around her.

As Ford watched, wave after wave of déjà vu blasted into him, as if every picture, letter, and postcard were calling to him with a story to tell—or show him. His knees wobbled, his vision darkened. Ford grabbed the edge of the computer desk to steady himself. No way did he want to pass out in front of Marie-Claire. He shook his head, trying to clear the haze.

Gavin grabbed his elbow. "You okay, Little Brother?"

Ford smiled, weakly. "Yeah, sure. I'm fine."

Ellie, still engrossed in her document search, finally waved a piece of paper above her head. "Here! It's a letter to the Royal Canadian Air Force." She skimmed through the letter. "Ford, Gavin, it's from your mom. She wanted to get his war records unsealed and it's dated just last year." Ellie continued reading.

Mrs. May MacKenzie
354 Augustina Bay
Winnipeg, Manitoba
R3Q 1H0

To Whom It May Concern,

I am looking for information regarding my Grandfather, Edward Hugh Martin Crawford. He was a pilot with the Royal Canadian Air Force in World War 2 and was discharged a Wing Commander in 1946 and was awarded the Member of the British Empire (MBE) Military Medal. We would like access to his war records.

Ford shifted his weight. "And?"

"They said no." She pointed to the word "DENIED" stamped in red on an angle across the top of the paper.

Gavin leaned over her shoulder and scanned the letter. "Does it say why?"

"No, but it says they've resealed his records for 'an undetermined period of time.'"

"Can I see that?" Ford asked.

Ellie pulled the letter closer to her body and out of Ford's reach and whispered, "Here? Are you sure? Will it be safe?"

"Why are you suddenly so concerned? I thought you doubted me."

"Well…I…" Ellie sighed. "I'm torn. Part of me thinks psychic stuff isn't real, but then another part of me—the part that has seen you in action thinks you really are a clairvoyant. I want to believe Mme. Bellerose. Honest."

"If you can't believe her, can't you just try to believe me? I am telling you this is part of who I am. I don't fully understand how it works, it just does."

Ellie nodded. "Okay, I'll try."

Gavin grabbed the letter out of Ellie's hand. He smiled at Marie-Claire. "We just need a few moments." He led them to the side of the library, where they couldn't be overheard. Ellie leaned against a stack of leather-bound books. Gavin frowned. "Ford, Marie-Claire can't know about you. We can't have her witness one of your visions. Remember what Mme. Bellerose said. We're supposed to protect you and be careful who we tell about your abilities."

"She also said to trust my instincts and my instincts say we can trust Marie-Claire."

"Are you sure it's your instincts and not your hormones?" Ellie asked, peering over Ford's shoulder towards Marie-Claire.

Ford rolled his eyes. "No, that is ridiculous."

Gavin held tightly to the letter. "Ford, I'm not sure—"

"Gavin. Please. I'm your brother. I have a good feeling about her."

Gavin shook his head. "Fine. But I'm not happy about this."

Ford took a deep breath and exhaled. "Just trust me."

CHAPTER 14

Marie-Claire nodded her head once they finished explaining Ford's clairvoyance abilities. "My grand-mère had a cousin, Amelie, and everyone said she had the second sight. There are many things we still do not understand in this world."

"I'm glad you aren't freaking out. I'm not sure everyone would be so calm hearing I can see the past," Ford said. "But I had a feeling you'd understand."

"And it's really important that you don't tell anyone. Ever," Gavin added.

"I will not. Your secret is safe with me."

"We trust you," Ford said. "Now, we need to find out more about this letter. It may hold the answers we need."

Ellie perched on the edge of the desk and stared at Ford. She handed him the letter.

He closed his eyes, counted to three, and then opened them. The library slowly faded out of sight and a high-backed, chocolate-brown leather armchair mater-ialized two feet in front of him. A large, dark wood desk slowly emerged on the other side of the chair. The desk top was perfectly tidy, seemingly with everything in its place—just like Gavin's bedroom desk at home.

He swallowed as his vision greyed and refocused. Every molecule of moisture evaporated from his mouth. The sounds of the library faded. The hum of an overhead light buzzed louder. A pungent smell made his eyes water. He rubbed at them, blinking. When he opened his eyes fully, a man with a grey buzz cut sat at the desk, with his back to Ford. How did that guy sneak in so fast? Ford hadn't heard a door open or footsteps cross the linoleum floor. Goosebumps rose across his skin once more. He wasn't sure he'd ever get used to this.

Ford cleared his throat. The man didn't flinch. Ford stood, stepped closer, and coughed, ready for the stranger to spin around and catch him spying. Nothing happened. "I wonder," Ford murmured and touched the chair. His fingers slid through the brown leather and disappeared. Warm tingles drifted up Ford's arm. He jerked his arm back. "Whoa!"

He examined every inch of the back of his hand and between his fingers. He flipped it over to inspect his palm. It looked totally normal. Ford clenched it as the zinging sensation dissipated. Weird.

Ford inspected the man. Who was he? Across each of the man's shoulders was a golden military insignia. It was jam-packed with emblems. Maybe this fellow was a lieutenant or a general. The officer placed a smoking cigar in a tarnished brass ashtray and leaned forward.

Ford stepped to the side, peering around the officer. In the man's hand was a letter, but Ford wasn't close enough to read the writing. He bent forward, intending to lean on the desk, but his hands passed through the wood. He lurched forward, stumbling. He regained his balance and stood in the desk.

In. The. Desk.

His heart raced. From mid-thigh down, all he could see was tabletop. No knees. No ankles. No toes. Just solid wood. Wait, not solid wood, more like… *air wood?* Was this some sort of mirage or illusion? Warmth washed over his feet and crashed up his calves. As it poured over his kneecaps, he staggered backward, away from the rolling heatwave.

"That was too weird," he mumbled, standing next to the officer. *I gotta be way more careful. No way do I want to fall into anything else.* He gasped. *Or into anyone!* He wiped his sweaty hands on his pants.

The officer placed the letter next to a thick file folder and pounded it with a wooden-handled stamper. Red-inked words popped from the page.

"Denied," Ford whispered. "Just like Mom's letter!" His gaze tracked down the document, right to the signature. *Mrs. May MacKenzie.* This was Mom's letter!

Pushing the letter to the side, the officer slid the folder closer. The words TOP SECRET were emblazoned across the cover. Now this was getting interesting. The man flipped it open, revealing a black-and-white picture paper-clipped to the inside cover of the folder. It was of a young man in uniform. Ford squinted, zooming in on the photo. Written below it was *E.H. Crawford.*

Our great-grandfather!

In another photo below it, he was in civilian clothes and he looked like he did in Ford's vision of *Les Deux Magots Café*. Running down the side of the folder was some sort of serial number. If only he shared Ellie's elephant-like memory. Ford figured she could read a telephone number once and remember it for the next twenty years. The only way Ford could commit something to memory was to write it out several times or recite it over and over until it sunk in.

"SOE: Crawford, E.H.M. #C00625," Ford repeated it three more times, hoping he wouldn't mix up the numbers.

The officer pulled out a stack of photos from the file and spread them across his desk. They were pictures of people who each had a gunshot wound to their forehead.

"Wait!" Ford cried. What had happened to those people?

The general pulled out one final photo of a woman who had been beaten, her eyes vacant. Déjà vu thrummed through Ford's entire body. His stomach recoiled. He felt like he was going to be sick. He snapped his eyes shut. He couldn't look anymore. He reared back and lost his footing and tumbled to the ground. His right hand smacked the floor.

"Ford! Ford!" A voice called. It was Ellie.

His eyes flashed open. He blinked hard, trying to stop his vision from swirling. His head spun. Ellie's face loomed close. His stomach swirled. Good thing he hadn't had that cheeseburger.

"What...what happened?" Ford asked,

"*Tu es tombé de la chaise*," Marie-Claire's words tumbled out, her face flushed. She scanned the library, then knelt next to Ford on the library's hardwood floor. "I mean, you—you fell out of the chair, but before that you went into some sort of trance." Her lavender perfume floated over Ford.

"*Oui*," he said, as Gavin helped him back into the chair. "Having a vision is kind of like being in a trance."

Ellie picked up the letter that had fluttered from Ford's hand when he tumbled to the floor. "Tell us what happened to you. What did you see?"

"And please, *mes amis*, lower your voices. We cannot disturb the other *bibliothèque* patrons."

Images flooded Ford's memory. "Right. I was in a room I'd never seen before and when I touched the furniture, poof, I'd suddenly be *in* the furniture. It was like everything around me was there, but not there." Ford scratched his head. It was really hard to explain something when you didn't fully understand it yourself.

Ellie grabbed her phone from her backpack on the floor. "Let me write this down. You can see everything and..."

"And I can smell things."

"But you can't touch anything."

"Sounds like Ford isn't meant to interact with anyone while he is having these visions," Gavin said.

"I think I'm supposed to be more of a witness, so I can learn something that happened in Great-Granddad's past. It feels like what I am seeing is important. Like my job is to put together everything I see like pieces of a puzzle. Just like Mme. Bellerose said."

Ellie cleared her throat. "Okay. This is really happening. Anything else?"

Gavin nodded. "Tell us everything."

Marie-Claire slid her glasses off and placed them high on her head like a hairband. She looked from Ellie to Gavin and then to Ford. Ford couldn't begin to imagine what she was thinking.

He exhaled slowly. "Okay, here goes. There was this military guy, I think he was pretty high ranked, and he had a file on Great-Granddad. In that file were these old black-and-white photos. A few of Great-Granddad and—" He gulped. "There were these other pictures. Horrible pictures of people—*dead* people. Each one had been shot. Except for one." Ford couldn't continue. He covered his face with his hands.

"Ford, it's okay," Ellie said, her voice unusually soft and gentle. "You don't have to tell us."

He sat up and looked right into Ellie's eyes. "No, I have to. I think it's important."

Ellie smiled a tiny smile and squeezed his shoulder. "Just take it slow."

"This woman, her face…" Ford closed his eyes and he could see the photo as clear as it had been in his vision. "One eye was swollen shut, with bruises that ran down that entire side of her face, and her hair had been shaved off—in patches. She was in a lot of pain."

"How do you know she was in pain?" Gavin asked.

"I-I dunno. Just a feeling. I felt a connection to her but not to any of the other people in the photographs."

Ellie slowly nodded her head. "Well that fits. Mme. Bellerose did say to trust your instincts and that you'd only have a connection to certain people."

"Is there anything else you can tell us?" Gavin asked.

"Well..." he paused. There was something he was supposed to remember—the serial number! Ford leaped off the chair, searching Marie-Claire's desk top for a pen and paper. He had to write it down before he forgot. "There was this number. It was written on a file. S.O.E:—"

"—Crawford, E.H.M. #C00625," Ellie said it along with him.

"How do you know the number?"

"You repeated it four times. It's the only thing you spoke clearly."

"You heard me?"

"Every word you uttered," Gavin said. "But you mumbled at first, so it was hard to understand most of what you said."

"*Mes amis,*" Marie-Claire's voice trembled. "I am worried for you. This S.O.E., it is not a child's game."

"What do you know about this S.O.E.?" Gavin asked Marie-Claire.

"S.O.E. stands for Special Operations Executive," Marie-Claire said. "It was one of the most important spy agencies in operation during the war."

Ellie leaped from her seat and pointed to the history books. "Yes! It popped up all over the place when I was paging through these books." Her smile widened. The tension slipped from Ford's shoulders. Ellie grabbed a text and flipped it open. Her finger ran down the chapter titles. "Here!" She flicked through it, then bounced on her tiptoes, book in hand, her eyes sparkling as she scanned the page. "It says they were a top-secret resistance organization and during the war few people even knew they existed! It's also known as 'Churchill's Secret Army' or the 'Ministry of Ungentlemanly Warfare.'"

"The Ministry of Ungentlemanly Warfare! That sounds like something out of Harry Potter," Ford said. "That is so cool!"

Ellie walked toward Ford. "Churchill's Secret Army. That means he did something dangerous." The smile disappeared from Ford's face as she stood inches from him. Her eyes seemed to bore right into Ford's own. "Very dangerous."

CHAPTER 15

Ellie read the S.O.E. number to Marie-Claire and in a blur Marie-Claire's fingers danced across the keys.

They stared at the computer screen. Gavin frowned. "That's it? Just two entries?"

"I am afraid so," Marie-Claire replied.

The screen flickered and went blank white. Ford leaned forward. "What happened?"

Marie-Claire jiggled the mouse. The screen remained blank. "I don't know. I've never seen this."

"Bad internet connection?" Ellie asked.

Marie-Claire frowned. "It could be this computer or a connection issue. We need to try a different computer."

"You can use mine," Ford said, unzipping his backpack. He pulled out his laptop and passed it to her, detaching his power cord, which he placed on the desk.

"*Merci,*" she said, as she flipped the computer open. It quickly blinked to life. "Let me open your internet browser and…it appears the problem is with the library computer. Let's try once more."

Marie-Claire typed in their great-grandfather's information and the moment the results appeared, Ford's laptop screen flashed, just like the library computer's had, and went white.

"Uh-oh," Ford said. "Now what?"

"Do you mind if we reboot it?" Ellie asked, pointing to the still-frozen library computer. "I want to try something."

"Sure." Marie-Claire moved from her chair so Ellie could sit down. "What do you think is wrong?"

"It may not be a computer problem. Maybe it's what we're searching for that's the problem."

"What? How does that make sense?" Ford asked.

Gavin crossed his arms. "Ellie's onto something. Everything was working fine, but as soon as we typed in S.O.E. and Great-Granddad's serial number, both computers locked up. You should reboot yours too, Ford."

"Yeah, that's a weird coincidence." Ford turned his laptop off.

"But what if it isn't a coincidence? What if—" said Gavin, but he stopped with a jump as a deep voice rumbled behind them.

"*Excusez-moi.* What are you doing?"

It was the rude librarian who ditched the cousins for lunch! His nose wrinkled as he stared at Ford, Ellie, and Gavin. Just like earlier. Surely they didn't actually smell. Ford resisted the urge to sniff-test his breath.

"*Oh, pardon Monsieur.* I am assisting these patrons with some research," Marie-Claire answered, her face flushed bright red.

"Mademoiselle LaFleur, how often must I remind you?" he said, his moustache twitching. His index finger tapped his pursed lips as he shook his head and tsk'd.

"Oh dear," Marie-Claire whispered. "*Monsieur, excusez-moi.*"

Monsieur Bouchard inhaled, his lips further pursing. He now resembled a man-sized goldfish. He slowly released his breath. He snapped his fingers and pointed to the high counter.

"No patrons on this side of the divide. *Vite, vite.*"

"Okay, okay," Ford muttered, stuffing his laptop into his bag as Ellie and Gavin scooped everything on the floor into Ellie's backpack. "We're hurrying already."

"Mademoiselle, a few moments, *s'il vous plait,*" Monsieur Bouchard said and guided Marie-Claire by the elbow to the far corner of the information booth, out of earshot.

"This guy is a serious control freak," whispered Ellie. "Poor Marie-Claire."

"He'd be the worst boss ever," agreed Ford. "Do you think she's in trouble?"

Gavin pointed to Marie-Claire, who was walking towards them. "Guaranteed."

"What do you think he said to her?" Ford whispered as Monsieur Bouchard turned on his heel and climbed the spiral staircase that led to the second floor.

"I dunno, but it can't be good. Look how pale she is," Ellie said.

Ford glared at Monsieur Bouchard's retreating back. "He's a complete fun-sucker."

"*Mes amis,*" Marie-Claire said. "Forgive me. I must return to my work."

"I hope we didn't get you into trouble," Ford said.

"Do not worry. It is just—"

"Your boss is a grouch. You didn't do anything wrong," Ellie said, interrupting Marie-Claire.

"Ah, *ma chérie*. He is not always right, but he is in charge. So, we find a way to work around his rules." She straightened her back, tossed her hair over her shoulders, and smiled. "Please take my business card." Her voice was low and determined. "If you need me, please call or return, but that would be best when Monsieur Bouchard is at lunch."

"Thank you for all your help," Ellie said.

"It is my pleasure. You are very sweet. I hope you find some answers. *Au revoir*." She kissed Ellie on both cheeks and waved to the boys.

"*Au revoir*," said Ford wishing Marie-Claire would hug him goodbye as well.

"Wow," Gavin whispered. "She was sure nice."

"So nice," Ford agreed.

"Good grief," Ellie muttered as she walked towards the library doors. "Seriously. How am I related to you two?"

Ford sped past her and out the doors. Ellie, close on his heels, frowned at the darkening sky. "Better run if we don't want to get drenched."

Heavy black clouds cast shadows across the pavement. The cousins sprinted through the parking lot towards the bus stop.

Ford kept pace with Ellie. "How long were we in the library?" he asked.

"Longer than Monsieur Bouchard liked, that's for sure. What a grump."

Gavin struggled to keep up as he looked at his watch. "It's 3:50. We have plenty of time to get back to the apartment before our parents get back."

Ford slowed as they approached the bus stop. "Can

you believe our great-grandfather was a spy? A real live undercover agent. Ministry of Ungentlemanly Warfare. How cool is that?"

Ellie nodded. "It is pretty cool. Now we just have to figure out why the air force refuses to release his war records."

Ford plunked down on a bench. "He must've done something pretty important." Ellie sat next to him.

"And dangerous," Gavin added, puffing. He massaged his side. "Remember what Marie-Claire said. 'The S.O.E. is not a child's game.'"

Across the street, a patch of blue broke through the clouds in the sky above the Pantheon and a sunbeam streamed down across the stairs. Colourful banners showcasing the latest art show hung between the tall marble pillars. A shadow of a memory tickled in Ford's mind. He closed his eyes and took a deep breath. There was something about that building. Something he needed to know. Now. He opened his eyes and stared at the Pantheon, trying to stop that déjà vu feeling from flitting away.

"Ellie, can I see the Pantheon stuff?" he asked.

"Sure. Just don't touch it."

She slid her bag from her shoulder and pulled out the stack of documents. She leafed through a half dozen or so before sliding out a letter. It was written on thin blue paper and was half the size of a piece of printer paper. "It's a letter from a Mr. W. Müller, but it's addressed to someone named Francis St. James."

She held it up in front of them, so Ford could see it. He leaned closer and squinted to decipher the handwriting. "Who the heck is Francis St. James and how is anyone supposed to read this?" He pointed at the slanted words.

Gavin moved to stand behind Ford and Ellie. He looked at the letter. "Handwriting, just like the English language, has changed a lot in the past seventy years." Ford's eyebrows shot up. "No kidding. Too bad they didn't have email."

Ellie flipped it around and cleared her throat. "It is pretty worn, but it's still fairly legible. *Dear Mr. St. James,*" she read out loud, "*...I regret to inform you... that I must cancel our engagement to attend the public reading of M. Chapeut's novel at the Pantheon at three o'clock. Please do let us reschedule our appointment.* It's dated January 3rd, 1944."

Dear Francis St James,   January 3rd, 1944

I regret to inform you that I must cancel our engagement to attend the public reading of Mr. Chapeut's novel at the Pantheon at three O'clock

Please let us reschedule our appointment.

Mr. W Müller

"Huh," Ford said. "Why would this note between these two people be important?"

Gavin pointed at the signature. "Look at the dots above the name Müller. Pretty sure that's a German last name."

Ford shrugged. "I guess, but what does this letter have to do with Great-Granddad?"

"Well…" Ellie began and thought for a moment. "There has to be a reason for him to have this, right? Maybe Francis St. James was a friend or a fellow spy."

"Maybe." Ford stared at it. "But if this Francis guy was a spy, then maybe he was meeting this German for secret information."

"That would make sense. Remember, Paris was occupied by Nazis by then, so it would've been extremely dangerous," Gavin added.

"Maybe Mr. Müller was their inside source," Ellie said.

"I think you may be right. That is what spies do, after all. They infiltrate enemy defences. We need to see if this letter has any real meaning." Ford took a deep breath. He let it out slowly. "We need to see if I get a vision when I touch it."

"Out here on the street? Are you sure?" Ellie asked.

Gavin wrapped his arm around Ford's shoulder. "He can do it." His brother sounded so certain that all Ford's doubt disappeared. He stood and dropped his backpack onto the bench seat.

Ellie stood in front of Ford. "Tell us everything you see and try to speak loudly so we can hear you.

No muttering this time. I'm going to take notes." She turned on her phone.

Once ready, she passed Ford the letter. He gripped it in both hands, as a now-familiar whispering of déjà vu flooded his senses. The paper slowly rippled in and out of focus, then vanished.

Ford looked across the street. The long art banners that draped between the pillars shimmered and faded. Long red flags slowly materialized in their place, becoming more vivid with each second. An instinctive shiver of fear snaked down Ford's spine as angry black swastikas appeared. Nazi flags.

Ford glanced down the street. Current-day pedestrians faded to mist, while German soldiers emerged from the gloom, taking their place. Nazis now stood at attention on every corner. Ford looked to the other end of the street. Only a few civilians remained and they were dressed in 1940s fashions: men in dark suits and fedoras, women in dresses with high heels and overcoats. All walked quickly with purpose, never making eye contact with the occupying force.

"Nazis," he said, remembering to speak clearly for Ellie. "Write this down. Nazis are everywhere. The French people look scared."

A military jeep slowed to a stop across the street. The driver jumped out and ran to open the door for the officer in the passenger side.

"I think an important German just arrived. Soldiers are saluting him." Ford watched the officer pull his cap low on his forehead as he dashed through the rain across the sidewalk and up the wide, wet stairs of the Pantheon. Rain. He held out his hand. The raindrops passed through. Ford felt nothing. "It's raining here. But I'm still dry."

A tall gentleman with a dark brown fedora stood at a newsstand near the end of the block. He kept glancing over his shoulder, first one way then the other.

"Ellie, there's this older guy, maybe forty years old and he's in a brown suit. He looks super nervous, like someone's watching him. Or maybe he's looking for someone." Or was Ford just imagining things? Maybe all this talk about spies had him paranoid.

Ford searched for similarities between the old photos he'd seen at home and the man he saw from his restaurant vision. "I don't think it's Great-Granddad."

A deep cough made Ford jump sideways as a man hunched into a black trench coat stepped past him. The man coughed much louder this time and made a great show of opening a large black umbrella. Ford gawked at the man in front of him.

"Come along, Wilhelm. Gotta keep moving," the man muttered under his breath. *Could it be?* The man glanced at Ford. His grey-blue eyes seemed to look right through Ford.

"You guys, I found him. Our great-grandfather is standing right in front of me!"

CHAPTER 16

Ford reached with trembling fingers towards their great-grandfather, his hand slipped through Great-Granddad's forearm, and disappeared up to Ford's wrist. Warmth spread up his arm, snaking towards his shoulder. He yanked his hand back. Pins and needles prickled his fingers, like they'd fallen asleep. His vision clouded, his head spun.

Note to self: avoid all contact with people when in the past.

Great-Granddad stared hard at the tall man at the newsstand. "Wilhelm. Put the paper down and follow me, you fool."

Ford smiled. "He talks to himself. A lot. And he sounds...gruff...no, not exactly gruff. More... irritated."

Finally, Wilhelm turned and bobbed his head in their direction. He folded his paper and stuffed it under his arm and strode their way.

Great-Granddad shook his head and sighed. "A complete imbecile, but you get what you get when there's a war on."

"Definitely irritated," Ford said loudly, so Ellie would hear.

Great-Granddad turned on his heel and began walking slow enough that Wilhelm could keep up, but fast enough that they didn't look like they were together.

"He's made contact with a man named Wilhelm," Ford said, keeping in step with him. They took a left down the first alleyway and immediately their great-grandfather sprinted through the narrow lane. Ford dashed after him, racing through mud puddles. He looked over his shoulder. Wilhelm ran too.

"We're running like mad now. I'm not sure where we're going."

They came to another alley and this time their great-grandfather turned right, only slightly slowing as he rounded the corner. Ford's feet pounded hard on the wet pavement.

"We're in a back lane, running between old buildings." Ford wanted to relay anything that might seem important later. "It really stinks, like rotten fish. We've come to a dead end, I'm not sure..."

Ford screeched to a halt and gawped as his great-grandfather leapt through the air and grasped onto the bottom rung of a rusted fire-escape ladder. He pulled himself up with what looked like little effort and climbed until he reached a wooden staircase zigzagging up the side of the building. He took the rickety stairs two at a time.

"He is ridiculous! He just scaled a fire escape like he was James Bond!"

As Ford considered how he was going to follow, Wilhelm flew past him, leaping through the air towards the metal rungs.

"Now that Wilhelm guy is doing it too! These guys would be perfect for *Cirque du Soleil*."

Ford reached up to the first rung of the ladder. His hand melted through the metal as Wilhelm's pounding footsteps echoed high above him.

"I'm falling behind." Ford hoped Ellie was taking accurate notes. "If I lose them, I won't find out why Wilhelm is important." And Ellie would never let him forget he messed up. "I'm not sure wh—" Ford gasped as he lifted off the ground. He lurched upwards as if a cord was attached to his chest pulling him through the air after the two men. He gained speed. The ladder rungs raced by faster and faster. His heartbeat raced in time.

What the…?

Right when Ford was sure his heart was going to burst through his chest, he pitched forward and skidded across a small cement landing, stopping only inches from the side of the building. With legs shaking, he stepped to the edge of the fire escape and peered over. It was a long way to the ground. What would've happened if he had fallen? Would he have died? He wasn't sure and no way did he want to find out. He took a deep breath, willing his heart to slow down.

"You guys are never going to believe this, but I just flew—like in the air—up the side of a six-storey building. There's an open doorway leading inside. Pretty sure that's where Great-Granddad and Wilhelm went."

He stepped inside and blinked to adjust to the dim light. A pungent smell of roasting garlic stung his nose. "They couldn't have gone too far."

Closed doors dotted the hallway in front of him, each one numbered, each one with a peephole. "I'm in an apartment block," Ford said. "The carpets are worn down to the floorboards." He picked up his pace and quickly travelled the length of the hall and sailed around a corner and right through Wilhelm. Tremors arced through his entire body. Heat engulfed him. Ford shook his legs and arms, hoping to return normal sensations to his limbs.

"That was gross. I just—" Ford paused. "Wilhelm is giving Great-Granddad a light brown envelope."

Was he watching spies in action? What could be in that envelope?

Great-Granddad tucked it into his inside jacket pocket and pulled out a folded slip of blue paper and held it in front of Wilhelm's face. "I can't express this strongly enough, Wilhelm. You must be more careful. This note you sent me could've exposed our entire mission. Agents, many agents, are at risk."

"*Ja. Ja.* I understand Francis," Wilhelm replied, his words heavily accented. Ford stared at the letter. It wasn't old or stained, but he still recognized it.

"Great-Granddad is holding the letter we used to see this memory and Wilhelm just called him Francis, which means...Great-Granddad is Francis!" Ford yelled. "It must be his undercover alias."

Wilhelm removed his hat. Wisps of toffee-coloured

hair framed his head in a circle, making him resemble a monk.

"I too have much at stake. My wife, my children…" He pulled a kerchief from his lapel pocket and wiped perspiration from his balding head, then carefully folded the cloth and placed it back in his pocket. He held his hat at his waist, his fingers clenched the brim, misshaping the fedora.

"Yes, I know. We have not forgotten your sacrifices." Great-Granddad's eyes tracked Wilhelm's every movement. Wilhelm did not raise his head. Great-Granddad's gaze did not leave Wilhelm's hands. Ford could feel tension radiate from Wilhelm.

Wilhelm cleared his throat. "*Gut. Gut.* I must go now."

"Wait, Wilhelm. Before we part. Tell me again of your children. I miss my own terribly. What were their names? Helga and…" His brows knit together. "Hans?"

"Yes, that is it. Helga and Hans."

"And…how are they?"

"They are good, yes. Very good children."

"Are they enjoying school?" He leaned towards Wilhelm, his head cocked to the side, eyebrows high.

Ford frowned. "I think he's interrogating Wilhelm. I don't think Great-Granddad trusts him."

Wilhelm paused before answering. "*Ja, ja.* They are very good pupils."

"How old are they? My memory is somewhat shoddy."

Wilhelm stepped back. "These questions I have answered before. Furthermore *Mr.* St. James, you have a perfect memory."

Great-Granddad tipped his head back and laughed. "Well, for most things yes, my memory is impeccable. But for some reason the details regarding your children escape me. Do they attend a Berlin school?"

"*Nein*. They are in the countryside with my wife's family. It is safer."

"Yes, it would be. Just like the schoolchildren in London, shipped out of the city to keep them out of harm's way."

"*Ja. Kinderlandverschickung*—relocation of the children to the countryside."

"Yes. And in order for us to keep them safe, we need to know their exact location."

Wilhelm nodded his head, his fingers digging deeper into his hat.

Ford stepped closer. "Wilhelm sounds German and he seems to be getting more and more nervous. For some reason, Great-Granddad is asking about Wilhelm's kids. I don't think Wilhelm wants to answer."

The German shifted his weight from one foot to the next. The floor creaked. "They are in school in D-Dresden," he said, stumbling over his words.

Great-Grandfather smiled. It was not friendly. "That is in Saxony, correct?"

Wilhelm nodded in response.

"Beautiful country."

Wilhelm only nodded again. He was beginning to resemble a bobblehead figurine. "I must be going." He looked down the hall towards the fire exit.

"Yes, as must I. Until we meet again, old chap." He clasped Wilhelm's hand and shook it firmly. "And

Wilhelm, please know how truly important you are to the war effort."

"*Ja. Ja.* Farewell, Francis."

"Wilhelm's leaving and Great-Granddad's just standing there watching him go. I'm not sure if he is going to follow Wilhelm or not."

Wilhelm disappeared down the stairwell before their great-grandfather moved. He sighed and a shadow passed over him, his shoulders sagged. He stuffed Wilhelm's note into his side pocket then reached into his coat and removed the envelope and tore it open. Ford stepped closer. His great-grandfather held a photo.

"General Carl-Heinrich von Stülpnagel. Let's hope this intel was worth the risk," Great-Granddad murmured and stuffed the package back in his pocket. "So many lives at stake."

He turned abruptly and stepped into Ford. A heatwave burned through Ford's entire body. It was like standing in the centre of the sun. A brilliant white light filled his vision, blinding him.

"Nooooo!" Ford stumbled forward and escaped his great-grandfather's aura. Like a lamp switched on, his sight returned. He shook his arms and legs, hoping to shake out any leftover dead man spirit or—whatever—from his body. Ford's legs trembled. His face dripped with sweat. He glanced down the hallway, expecting to see his great-grandfather. It was empty. He spun around.

"He's gone! He just vanished!" Ford raced in the last direction Great-Granddad had gone. The hallway dimmed, the walls slowly dissolved. Sunlight filtered through the greyed corridor, erasing all shadow. Cement replaced the carpeting under his feet.

"Noooo!" he cried. "Come back!"

Ford spun around, looking for Wilhelm or Great-Granddad and found only Ellie and Gavin staring back at him.

"Hey, calm down. Everything is okay," Gavin said.

"What? But—I wasn't done." Ford glanced down the Paris street. His legs were like jelly. "I'm back."

"Technically, you never actually left," said Ellie.

"But I just raced down alleyways and flew up the side of a fire escape."

"But back here in reality, you never left the sidewalk," Ellie said.

Ford looked at his feet, expecting them to be plastered with mud from splashing through puddles. They were dry and nearly perfectly clean. A cool breeze tussled his hair, the letter flapped in the wind. The letter. It was still in his hand.

"You did a lot of running on the spot and leaping in the air," Gavin said. "We were able to stop you from jumping into the street and you got a lot of strange looks."

Ellie laughed. "That's for sure. Gavin told people you were a street performer."

Ford slumped onto the bus-stop bench, next to his backpack. "It felt so real."

"Are you okay?" Gavin leaned down to examine Ford. His gaze darted across his face, settling on his eyes.

"Yeah, I guess. I just feel strange." His arms and legs ached and he felt like he was running a fever. His stomach gurgled. "And I am starving."

Ellie laughed. "I don't have any food, but I took lots of notes. This time I could understand every word you said. Francis St. James—an actual alias. For sure he was a secret agent and I bet this Colonel von Stülpnagel is important. I think we uncovered the beginning of Great-Granddad's wartime mystery."

"Yeah, but I was just getting to the good stuff." He knew he sounded whiney and he didn't care. "Maybe I can go back and look for more clues or follow Great-Granddad and find out more." He looked down at the frayed blue paper and flipped it over. Nothing. He passed it between his hands. Still nothing. Ford closed his eyes and took a long, deep breath.

Come on Great-Grandpappy. Do your thing!

Not even a glimmer of the vision. Disappointment, frustration, impatience flooded over him. "I don't understand. Why can't I see it again?"

"Maybe it's like a one-time-only ticket—like a movie ticket only gets you one viewing. If we, and when I say we I mean you not me, can only see each memory or vision or whatever it is once, we had better always be prepared," Ellie said.

"Right—prepared," Ford said. He stared at his hands. How could they look like they always did, when he had walked through some sort of great-granddad ghost?

"Hey, little brother, are you sure you're okay?" Gavin asked.

"Yeah, I—" Ford began, but stopped as their bus pulled up. They clambered onboard and flashed their passes under the scanner. In single file, they hurried to the back, to the only free seats. Ford sat closest to the window. "I still feel creeped out from when he walked through me."

Ellie grinned, sliding in next. "It is exceedingly creepy. What exactly did it feel like?"

Ford looked around the bus. He hoped not many of them could understand English. He leaned closer to Ellie and Gavin. "The first time I touched him, when I was on the street outside the Pantheon, just my hand got warm and tingly. That was a little uncomfortable, kind of like when you sit too long with your legs crossed and your foot goes to sleep. It was a little bit worse than when I fell into that desk in that other vision. Running through Wilhelm wasn't fun, but when Great-Granddad passed through me, it was different, way more intense. It was like my entire body was suddenly on fire, with electrical currents running up and down my arms, and then there was this bright white light. I couldn't see anything."

Ellie whistled. "That is totally freaky."

"Yeah, I know and you guys," Ford said quietly. He stared at his hands. They began to shake. The letter fluttered like a trapped butterfly. "I think it was his soul. I think our great-grandfather's soul passed through me."

Gavin looked at Ellie, his eyes wide. She swallowed but wouldn't look at Ford.

Beads of sweat broke out across Ford's nose. "Say something!" Ford's voice was high. "You both look like you think I'm nuts and I thought we agreed I was not."

Finally, Ellie looked at him. "It's just a lot to take in. Before today, I would've said all of this was impossible. Seeing the past, connecting with our very long-dead great-granddad, spies, covert missions—it's all hard to believe, but I know you and you're not crazy. What you're seeing is real, or at least your visions are real. Or..." Ellie shook her head. "Ugggh, this is all so confusing."

"Yeah, well try being the one it's happening to. It's not easy being the one who sees dead people. Well, sort of sees dead people, or the memories of dead people, or the souls of dead people or—whatever."

"Agreed. What we need, before you go on any more visions, is a plan," Gavin said.

Ford nodded. "I've been thinking about that. Remember when Mme. Bellerose held her hand above everything and then she told us we had to figure this out ourselves? She must have got some message telling her they were important, so I am going to try do the same thing. I'm going to see what I can find out before I take another journey into the past."

"Good idea," Gavin said.

Ellie frowned.

Ford sighed. "Listen, I know you are having trouble accepting all of this, but you said you were going to trust me and all I can tell you is, it just feels right. And remember, Mme. Bellerose told me to trust my instincts."

Ellie rolled her eyes. "Yeah, how could we forget? You've said it like fifty-zillion times."

"Ha ha ha. Very funny."

Ellie stood. "This is our stop."

They dashed off the bus and down to the end of the street to their apartment. Gavin yanked the large dark wood door open and, as Ellie stepped inside, Ford noticed a large black car inching along the road that ran perpendicular to them. Ford squinted, but it was difficult to see into the darkly tinted windows. *Was someone in the backseat staring at him?*

"Hey, guys!" Ford called, but the driver floored it and squealed around the corner.

Ellie popped her head out the doorway. "What?"

"It was, just—nothing," Ford shook his head. He was seriously getting way too paranoid. He had to remember it was his great-grandfather who was the great spy, not him.

His stomach grumbled louder. Ellie rolled her eyes.

"Only you would be hungry at a time like this."

"A time like this. What does that mean?"

"We're on the verge of piecing together Great-Granddad's mystery messages and all you can think about is eating."

"Hey...no fair! I can't help it if my body craves food."

"Fine. Let's grab a quick snack and get back to work."

"So no burgers and fries?"

Ellie swung her backpack and whomped him on the shoulder. He stumbled down the steps and landed hard on his rear end. Gavin snickered.

"I take that as a no?"

CHAPTER 17

"Meet in my room," Ford said as he raced down the hallway to the kitchen. "My stomach needs food."

He grabbed two dinner plates from the cupboard and laid them on the counter. "Quick and easy," he mumbled, as he rifled through the fridge. "Fruit, cheese, chocolate, and—" Ford slammed the door closed and scooted across the room to the pantry. "Chips!" He grabbed three small bags and threw them on top of the food platters.

"Snacks!" he called to Ellie and Gavin as he nearly ran back to his room. He kicked the bottom of his door. "Hey guys, open up."

The door opened as a chip bag slid from the pile and teetered on the edge of the plate. Gavin grabbed it and tore it open. "Thanks."

"Careful where you walk. We've spread out everything from Great-Granddad's briefcase for you to examine," Ellie said.

Ford narrowly missed stepping on an unfolded brochure of the Catacombs as he strode across his room. He set the food down on his desk and stuffed a wedge of brie in his mouth.

"There were fourteen items in the briefcase. You've already had three visions and there was the one that didn't work. That leaves us with ten more possibilities," said Gavin.

Ellie nodded. "And who knows which ones hold secrets and which ones are just duds."

"Well, I know. Or at least I will in a moment. I think," said Ford, his heart fluttering in his chest and his palms suddenly sweaty. "So, I think what I need to do is search for any déjà vu feelings, without touching anything."

"Sounds simple enough," Gavin said. He pointed to a second picture of the *Les Deux Magots*. This one had a deep crease down the middle, like it had been folded for decades. "Great-Granddad sure liked that restaurant."

Ford held his hand over the photo, closed his eyes, and relaxed his mind. "Keeper." He moved rapidly over the next four items. "Dud, keeper, keeper, dud," he said without hesitation.

His eyes flashed open. "This one makes me nervous." Ford nodded to a weathered Eiffel Tower postcard. A bead of sweat broke out along his hairline. He wiped the back of his hand across his forehead. Dread. That postcard was filled with dread.

Ellie patted Ford's back. "I can see it's frightening you, but I still hope it holds a vision. I mean, how cool would it be if Great-Granddad's past took us there?"

Ford held his hand above the postcard. Nausea rushed up his throat. He yanked his hand away and staggered backward. Gavin rushed to his side.

"Yup. It's loaded." Ford shuddered. "But I wish it wasn't. Something bad happened there."

Ellie bit her lip and gingerly picked the postcard up with two fingers, like it would taint her as it did Ford. She let out a long rush of breath as she placed it with the other visions.

Worry showed in every crease in Gavin's forehead. "I am almost afraid to ask you to continue, Ford. The look on your face..."

Ford squared his shoulders and stood tall, nodding to the next postcard. "I can do this." He closed his eyes. "Yup, it's a keeper and thankfully no sick feelings."

"Only three more," Ellie said.

He let out a sigh, his hand shook as he held it over another document. "Here we go. Dud and dud." He opened his eyes. "This last one is interesting."

"A bookmark?" Ellie asked, picking it up. She stared at the simple pencil sketch of the Notre Dame Cathedral. At the bottom, someone had handwritten a Bible quote in black ink. "*And then you shall know the truth, and the truth shall set you free*," Ellie read in a whisper.

"What truth? Is it referring to God...or something else?" Ford asked Ellie.

She shrugged. "I dunno."

Ford's hand wasn't even fully over the bookmark when an urgent rush of déjà vu flooded through his fingers and up his arm. "Yeah, that's a keeper. Something important happens there."

"Guess we have our plan all set for us," Ellie said.

"But where do we begin?" Gavin asked. "Logically we should be following Great-Granddad's footsteps in some sort of organized fashion."

"Do you think you can tell us that, too—where to begin?" Ellie asked Ford.

"Might as well try."

Where do we start?

A vision of *Les Deux Magots* materialized in his mind. His eyes flashed open. "We start at the café, then…" he closed his eyes. "I see the *Louvre* followed by the water fountains of the *Palais de Chaillot*." He looked across at Ellie, who stood on the other side of the bed. He wiped his hands on his jeans.

Within seconds the bookmark came into focus in his brain, "The Notre Dame Cathedral is our next stop, then…" he paused, a chill racing up his fingers. "The Eiffel Tower."

"That leaves the Catacombs as our final destination," Ellie said, putting them in order.

Ford stepped back, his head woozy.

"Are you okay?" Gavin asked.

"Yeah, just glad we're done."

"Done? Heck, we're just getting started," Ellie said, her eyes sparkling. She glanced from Ford to Gavin. "Come on you two, can't you just taste it?"

Ford frowned. "What are you talking about?"

"Adventure. There is adventure in the air."

"You are certifiable," Ford said.

"Most definitely," Gavin agreed.

Ellie rolled her eyes. "You wait, you'll see. This will be the most exciting thing we have ever done."

Ford nodded. He knew that determined look of his cousin and he knew it meant that arguing was not an option. He smiled. "Just nod and smile, Gav. Nod and smile."

"I'm moving all the Great-Granddad clues to my room for safekeeping," Ellie said, carefully bundling the keepers separately from the duds. "I'll quickly write some notes on my phone about these and put the rejects back into the briefcase, so we don't get anything mixed up."

Ford popped a potato chip in his mouth and sat on his bed as she scurried out of his room. Psychic work sure made him hungry. "Hey, Gav. Can you believe this? I mean, would you ever have imagined we'd be sitting here discussing clairvoyance, quantum physics, and secret agents?

Gavin moved Ford's backpack and sat cross-legged at the end of Ford's bed. "Not in a million years."

"And I gotta say, your brain is really coming in handy. You know, you would make a good teacher. You remember all sorts of trivial facts and you're getting better at explaining things so that people understand. Well, I understood you most of the time today." Ford laughed. "Although, you did stump me with that *Sum over Histories* stuff."

Gavin fiddled with the hem of his jeans. "Uhm, I have to tell you something."

"What's that?"

"Don't tell Mom and Dad, okay?"

"Okay."

"I sort of dropped out of university."

"What!?" Ford couldn't believe it. Gavin was the golden child when it came to school.

"Shhh. I don't want Ellie to know." Gavin peered at the open doorway. "At least, not yet."

"What happened? Why'd you quit?"

"I was just so lonely on campus and it was all too much. I love the academic side of university, but I was so homesick and I-I just didn't feel like I was doing the right thing for me."

Ford whistled as he unzipped his bag and pulled out his lap top. "You dropped out. That's huge."

"I know, and you kind of hit the nail on the head about the teacher thing. It's what I have always secretly wanted to be. I'd love to hook other kids onto math, science, history—everything. Maybe I could even be a professor like Mom and Dad someday."

"You'll be great at whatever you do, Gavin."

He tilted his head and looked at Ford. "You think?"

"Yeah, but you need to tell Mom and Dad. They won't be mad at you. They never get mad at you."

"I guess, but all they talk about is my 'limitless potential' and how much I am taking after Great-Granddad. It's a lot to live up to and a whole lot of studying." His hands fell in his lap. "They're going to be so disappointed."

Ford drummed his fingers on the top of his computer as he considered this.

"I never knew you felt that way. I sort of thought you were just like Great-Granddad too. I figured everything came easy to you, that everything was already in your brain, like a bank vault of intelligence and you just had to enter the code and presto, you had answers to everything."

"Part of that is correct. I can often figure things out really fast and sometimes it feels like I've always known it, but I still need to study. High school is nothing like university, in so many ways." Gavin sighed. "I still think I'll be letting them down."

"Even if they are a bit disappointed, they'll get over it. For parents, they are pretty cool. Even though they are mega nerdy. Plus, they are professors, so how can they argue with your dream of following in their footsteps?"

"Thanks Ford. You sure know how to make me feel better. I can't remember when I've felt so…happy."

"Yeah, well I guess we all have our talents." Ford reached to the bottom of his bag and pulled out scrunched-up pamphlets, gum wrappers, and three mismatched socks. He unzipped each side pocket. "I can't find it!"

"What are you looking for?"

"My power cord. I need it to charge my computer. Where did I leave it?"

"The only place you brought it out was—"

"The library!" they said in unison. The boys suddenly wore identical cheesy grins.

"We'll have to go back—" began Ford.

"Tomorrow. Agreed."

They high-fived as the apartment's front door creaked open.

"Kids! We're baaaaack!" Mom sang, her voice echoing down the hallway.

Ford and Gavin looked at each other and burst into laughter.

"Very, very nerdy," said Ford.

Gavin nodded, with a face-covering grin. "Very."

Ford thought he'd never seen his brother look so happy.

"How was your day?" Mom asked as she and Aunt June strolled into Ford's room, shopping bags hanging from their arms. Mom's sunglasses perched on the top of her head, half buried in a mound of red curls. Aunt June's glasses hung by a gold chain around her neck, her hair hidden under a rather floppy celery green-coloured hat.

Ellie bounded into the room, pecked her mom on the cheek, then dove onto the bed between her cousins. Gavin grabbed the bedpost so he wouldn't fall off.

"Dinner's in an hour. Your dads are making crepes," said Aunt June.

"And we are going to have a glass of wine on the balcony," added Mom. "And after dinner we are having a family meeting to plan out the rest of our week in Paris. Come with ideas. If there is someplace you want to see, let us know."

They linked arms, their eyes sparkling and smiles identical as they disappeared down the hallway.

"Race you to the kitchen," Ford said and dashed through the doorway, with Ellie and Gavin close on his heels.

"Cheater!" Ellie called.

"You mean, winner!" Ford said, laughing. He didn't think he'd been happier in his life. Another thing he had in common with his brother—utter happiness.

♦

Gavin flopped onto the couch in the living room. "Those were the best crepes, ever."

Ellie sat next to him, a napkin in her hand. "In the entire universe."

Ford sprawled in an overstuffed chair, his legs dangling over one of the plump arms. He moaned. "I think I ate one too many."

Ellie laughed. "Don't you mean you ate ten too many? I have no idea how you can eat so much and stay so skinny."

Uncle Jim sat in the chair opposite Ford and laughed. "I used to be like you son, I could eat all I wanted and more, then one day, ba-bam, I grew this big ol' belly. Now no amount of that rabbit food your Aunt June force-feeds me is shrinking my girth." Uncle Jim rubbed his rather large stomach.

"Oh dear, I love you just as you are," Aunt June said, as she perched on the chair's armrest. She draped her arm around his shoulder and gave him a smooch on the cheek.

He stared up at his wife, a look of pure adoration in his eyes. "Sugar Dumpling, you have a way with words."

"Oh brother. Old Person Romance. That should be outlawed," Ford muttered.

"All rightieooooo faaaaamily," Mom sang as she entered the room, her arms full of tourism pamphlets. "Time to plan our remaining days in Paris. We don't want to get to London with any regrets over missing something important."

"We have some ideas, too," Ellie said, waving her napkin in the air. "I have a list."

"When did you make that?" Gavin asked.

"At dinner when you and Ford were licking Crepes Suzette off your plates."

Uncle Jim winked at Ellie. "That's my Sweetpea. Always ready for everything."

"Let's have the kids go first," Dad said. "I'm curious to see what they have on their Paris list."

"Well, we'd like to see—" Ellie began.

Ford shot upright. "I have something to add!"

He zipped over to Ellie and whispered in her ear. "We need to return to the library to get my power cord. I forgot it there."

"Really. You *forgot* it?" she whispered back, rolling her eyes.

"It was an accident. Honest."

Ellie grunted. "Likely story." She scrawled it on the napkin in big, black, spikey letters, then passed it to Ford's mom. "Here you go."

"Wow," Dad said, peering over Mom's shoulder as she scanned the paper. "That is a lengthy must-see list."

"And we'd like to see them in that order. More or less," Ellie said.

Uncle Jim chuckled. "That's my girl. Organized down to the last detail."

"Many of the places you've listed are also on our checklist, so this may work quite well," said Mom, passing it to her sister.

"Looks good to me. The only conflict I can think of is tomorrow's boat tour, although we do have a choice of tours," Aunt June said, then spoke directly to the kids. "Currently, we are leaning towards one that follows Paris history through the past 600 years. This particular tour company is known for their comprehensive details."

"Ugh," mumbled Ford.

"What's that Ford?" Mom asked.

"Oh, I was just wondering how long the tour will take."

"Three hours. There was a four-hour voyage, but the only one they offered was in French and we didn't think that would be a good choice, given—"

"My poor French skills?" Ford finished, for once thankful that he wasn't as good as the rest of his family at foreign languages. "It is still a long time to be on a boat..."

"Yes, and there is a third option. Your dad thought you may prefer it," Mom said.

Dad winked at Ford. "The final option is a longer cruise, closer to five hours—"

Ford slumped back in his chair. "Five hours? Dad—"

"Wait, wait. I am not done. It is a longer cruise that docks partway, close to the Eiffel Tower. You three can disembark and tour around for a few hours while we continue, and we can meet up at the Louvre at 3:30 on the dot."

"We can do the library and café on our own, which you don't want to see. That's perfect," said Ellie.

"Yeah, it sounds great! Thanks," said Ford.

"Glad you're happy. Your dad was insistent on that third option. Now, it's time for you kids to head to your rooms for bed. It's late and we have an early start tomorrow. Everyone up at 6am shaaaaaaarp!" Mom singsonged.

Ford sighed. "She giveth with one hand and taketh with the other."

"What are you now? Some sort of psychic philosopher?" Ellie asked as they shuffled down the hall.

"Yup, that's me, Fordacle the Oracle. Rub my belly and I will tell you your future."

Gavin dropped his arm around Ford's shoulder. "I think you are getting mixed up with Buddha. Did you know, Buddha Shakyamuni was the first Buddha? He was born a royal prince in 624 BC and interestingly, the region where he was born was originally a part of Northern India, but now it is a part of Nepal..."

Ford smiled. He was getting to like this sixty-year-old man-child brother of his.

CHAPTER 18

Ford, Ellie, and Gavin stood at the front of the boat, a warm breeze ruffling their hair as the tour guide rattled on about all things Paris: Napoleon, the French Revolution, the history of Paris patiseries, and of course guillotines.

Ellie grimaced. "For such a beautiful city, it sure had a grisly past."

"History is pock-marked with murderous moments," said Gavin nodding, a smile dancing on his lips. He looked ready to dive into a full history lesson.

"Pock-mocked with murderous moments?" Ford teased.

Gavin's smile quivered, then disappeared. He lowered his head.

"Ford!" Ellie said.

Shame flamed through Ford as he watched his brother's face redden. Gavin hadn't always taken offence this easily. He cleared this throat. "Uhm... what I meant was that almost sounded like poetry. You make history interesting, Gavin."

Gavin peered at Ford. "You think so?"

"Yeah, I really do. You should be the one guiding this tour, instead of that boring old geezer." Ford pointed at the elderly tour guide who sat perched on a tall stool and had bellowed supposedly interesting facts into a megaphone for the past two hours. "I was only joking around."

Ellie wrapped her arms around her cousins' necks. "Now that's what I like to see: brotherly love."

"Don't get carried away. Gavin's still a colossal nerd."

"And you're still a huge pain in the—"

"Okay, okay. I get it; you're brothers, you fight," interrupted Ellie.

"Look! We're almost there." Gavin pointed at the Eiffel Tower which loomed ahead. "It seems so much bigger in real life."

"Here they come," Ford said, nodding at Uncle Jim and Dad as they wandered across the boat deck. A small French flag waved from the top of Uncle Jim's baseball cap.

Ellie laughed. "Look at my Dad. Such a tourist."

"Shhh! He'll hear you," Gavin said. "Hey Dad. Hey Uncle Jim."

"Hey yourself," Dad said. "Are you kids ready to take off?"

Uncle Jim smiled. "Ellie already filled me in on your plans."

Ford's breath caught. "She did what?"

Ellie leapt to Ford's side. "I sure did. We're off the library and then lunch at *Les Deux Magots* for their world-famous…croissantwiches and…chocolate mousse. I have our route all planned out."

Ford stared at his cousin. She stared back. World-famous croissantwiches? What was she talking about?

"Ellie—" Ford began, but Uncle Jim's booming voice cut him off and drowned him out.

"Lordy, Lordy, you are a marvel," Uncle Jim beamed at Ellie. "Leave it to my Sweetpea to have every moment of your day plotted and organized."

"And we're here!" Gavin said, shrugging his backpack onto his shoulders as the boat docked.

Dad peered over the rim of his glasses at Ford and Gavin. "Ah, right. *Au revoir,* boys. You have my number in case of emergency. Have fun and use your heads. Remember you are in a new city, so if something seems fishy, follow your gut. Your instincts won't often steer you wrong."

Funny, Mme. Bellerose had instructed Ford to do the same thing.

"Thanks Dad," Gavin said "No need to worry about us. As Ellie said, we've got it all planned out from start to finish."

The cousins raced down the plank to shore, weaving between masses of people. Snippets of conversations in French, Italian, English, Spanish, and a whole bevvy of other languages swirled around them. They broke free from the crowd and raced to the bottom of a wide, cement staircase that led to the street above—the *Quai Branly.*

"This way," Ellie said. She darted up the steps with Gavin and Ford close behind. Ford's heart beat wildly.

"So what was all that talk about sandwiches?" Ford asked her when they reached the top.

"Oh, yeah. My dad basically interrogated me last night when he came to say goodnight. He couldn't figure out why two middle-schoolers and a university student were so taken with a military library and a café frequented by artists. I had to do some fast talking to get him to back down."

"That was pretty good thinking," Gavin said.

"Yeah, well you can thank me later. Now we have a mystery to unravel."

Ellie showed Ford and Gavin the map on her phone. "We have a bit of a journey ahead of us and we are on a tight schedule. So, we need to get your power cord and get to our first destination—*Les Deux Magots Café*—as fast as we can. That means no extra chatting with your wannabe girlfriend, Marie-Claire." Ellie poked Ford in the ribs.

"Stop it," Ford grabbed her fingers and shoved her hand away. "And what do you mean, wannabe girl-friend? I have no idea what—"

"Zip it. Just listen. Grab your power cord and then we fly. Remember, whatever happens, we can't be late meeting our parents at the Louvre. 3:30 sharp means not one second late to The Sisters. If we're past our meeting time, they are going to tan our hides and they might get suspicious. We cannot afford suspicious parents. Especially after my dad's interrogation last night."

"True. How far is it from the café to the Louvre?" Gavin asked.

Ellie typed on her phone. "We can walk there in fifteen minutes. So as long as we leave the café by 3:10, we'll have plenty of time."

Ford looked out the window at the Eiffel Tower as they pulled away from the curb. "See ya later, tower." He pulled his phone out of his pocket. "Hello Monster Madness. Time to level up."

Ford smiled as he shifted in his seat, ready for thirty minutes of uninterrupted gaming time. *Vive la France!*

CHAPTER 19

Marie-Claire raced across the library floor towards them. Her heels clicked fast and loud, her face pale, a look of fear in her eyes. This was not the same happy, rosy-faced Marie-Claire they had met yesterday.

Her words tumbled out before they could even say hello. "There was a man and a woman, and they were looking for you this morning. I think the woman may still be here. I didn't see her leave, but I've been busy cataloging books so I can't be certain. You need to leave. It is not safe for you."

"What?" Ford asked, confused. What man and woman? Marie-Claire wasn't making any sense. "Who would be looking for us?"

She looked over her shoulder, then back at Ford. "You must go. You cannot be seen. Please, hurry." She grabbed his hand and pulled him toward the wall of books on the side of the great room. "*Vite, vite,*" she said to Ellie and Gavin, her voice barely above a whisper. Her stride quickened. Ellie and Gavin kept pace.

She dropped Ford's hand and lifted a keyring from her suit-jacket pocket. Unlocking a door partially obscured by a wall of books, she turned a darkened brass knob and led them into a maintenance hallway. It was dim, only lit by bare bulbs that hung every ten feet or so along the ceiling. A bright green *SORTIE* sign shone at the end of the hallway. Once all three cousins passed through the doorway, Marie-Claire closed the door and locked it. She let out a long, shaky breath.

"These people, they spoke to Monsieur Bouchard at great length and then they asked me so many questions—questions about all three of you: why you came to the library, what you were looking for, and"—she glanced at Ford—"many, many questions about you."

A lump of fear formed in Ford's throat. Why would anyone come looking for him? Mme. Bellerose's warning came to mind. He had no intention of becoming anyone's agent of evil. "And what did you say?"

Ellie gently took Marie-Claire's hands and looked directly into her eyes. "Did you tell them about Ford's abilities?" Ellie whispered, urgency lacing each word.

Marie-Claire shook her head, her voice wobbling as she answered. "No. No, I kept his secret, but they knew so much already. I got the feeling they already knew you were searching for information about your great-grandfather, they just wanted me to say it."

"How could they know?" Ford asked.

Marie-Claire removed her glasses and cleaned them on her blouse. "I think our computer search on your great-grandfather triggered an alarm...of sorts."

"An alarm? Like a fire alarm?" Ellie asked.

"No, quite the opposite. A fire alarm is intended to warn the public of danger. What I am referring to is a silent alarm designed to warn an elite few of danger or discovery."

"An elite few, or…entire governments," Gavin added. "It is common knowledge that governments have their secret service agencies monitor what people search on the internet. I guess that means we're being watched now."

"But why would anyone care about a bunch of kids googling a long-dead relative?" Ford said.

Marie-Claire sighed. "I suppose that is the question you must answer. I fear you have awoken a sleeping dragon. You must remember that there is a reason that people say war is hell. Things happen; people, soldiers, civilians, and governments do things that they would not do during peace time. What I learned in my university studies is that there are some war secrets governments do not want the public to discover, even decades later."

What had Great-Granddad been involved in? Fear stirred deep inside of Ford. It churned in his belly. Did he really want to know?

"So who exactly were those people who came looking for us?" Ellie asked.

Marie-Claire shook her head. "That isn't so easy to say. Logically, you should explore secret service agencies related to your initial search."

"You think spies are after us?" Ellie said.

"That is the most likely conclusion," Gavin said.

Marie-Claire nodded. "They were definitely not gendarmes. The man who spoke to me had an English accent. The woman never uttered one word."

"English accent...would they be from the Special Operations Executive? That's who we searched up. Are they even still around?" Ellie asked.

"Well, sort of. They officially ceased to exist after the war, but their...*contre-renseignement*...counter-intelligence work would have been carried out by Britain's secret service agency—MI6," Marie-Claire explained.

"Britain's secret service. So, we could have a 007 after us?" Ellie asked. Ford could hear a thrill of excitement in her voice.

Marie-Claire smiled at Ellie. Her lips trembled. "Yes, and they often share information with their partners in America. Which means, those operatives could also be CIA."

"What about Canadian secret service? Our great-grandfather was Canadian after all," Gavin asked.

Marie-Claire tilted her head, her shoulders lifted. "Yes, perhaps. There are many unseen alliances between the military and the secret service and amongst nations, so I suppose anything is possible."

Ellie looked at Ford. "Okay, fearless leader. Now what?"

Good question. When Mme. Bellerose said he was going to be a great clairvoyant, she never mentioned he'd also have to dodge spies as they retraced Great-Granddad's footsteps. It would have been nice for her to have given them a bit of a warning. "I...I guess we just...keep our eyes open for spies and get to the café to see if my next vision gets us closer to unravelling Great-Granddad's past."

"That is your plan? A real-life game of I Spy?" Ellie asked.

What did she expect from him? A step-by-step user's guide to outrunning spies?

"Do you have a better plan?"

"Sadly, no."

Marie-Claire's phone pinged. She tapped open a message, her face glowing in the screen's light. "I must go. Monsieur Bouchard has noticed my absence. You can safely depart through that exit door. I will make my way through the hidden hallways and return to the library on the opposite side, in case my supervisor is watching for me."

"Thank you, Marie-Claire, and thank you for warning us," Ellie said.

"And sorry we got you involved…in whatever it is we are involved in," Ford said.

"You must not return. I know I gave you my business card yesterday, but if you do need to contact me, it may be safer if you text me on my mobile." Marie-Claire scrawled a long number on the back of another card and passed it to Ford. "Be careful. Trust no one."

"Except you," Ford said, blushing.

Marie-Claire smiled. "Yes, except for me. I shall always keep your secret." Her phone pinged again, echoing around them. "Now go."

Ellie snatched the card from his hand and slipped it into a side pocket of her backpack. "For safekeeping," she explained.

Silently the cousins tiptoed towards the *sortie* —exit—sign.

Trust no one. Mme. Bellerose's exact same warning.

Ellie darted through the back doors of the library with Gavin close behind. Ford stopped at the top of a small, metal staircase as Ellie and Gavin clanked down the steps. "You guys! I didn't get my power cord!"

Ellie moaned as she reached the pavement.

"Do you think I should go back?" Ford asked.

"No!" Gavin and Ellie said in unison.

"You can always borrow mine," Gavin offered.

"Right." Ford hesitated before continuing. "Do you think Marie-Claire will be okay?"

"Yeah, she's pretty tough," Gavin said.

"Gavin's right. I was actually really impressed by her. She is a warrior woman," Ellie said.

"That's true, I—" Ford's neck bristled with a sense that someone was watching them. He turned quickly, looking out across the parking lot for a set of prying eyes. "Just a bunch of empty cars," he murmured. Then his gaze stopped on a black sedan, two rows back. A man with sunglasses sat behind the wheel. A woman sat next to him. She had a camera with a long telephoto lens and she was taking pictures— *of Ford*.

They *were* being followed! A shiver snaked across his shoulders and rippled down his spine.

"Hey, you coming?" Gavin called from the sidewalk below.

Ford's mouth dried, making talking difficult. He pointed towards the car. "Someone's spying on us."

Ellie spun in the direction Ford pointed. "Spying? Where?"

Ford nodded to the dark car and tore down the stairs. "There are two people over there taking pictures of us. Wh-what are we going to do?"

Gavin shoved Ford behind him. "You stay out of sight."

Ellie stepped next to Gavin, standing in her mock-karate pose. "We have to lose them."

"How?" Ford asked, fear leached into every cell of his body. What would happen if they caught him? No. He couldn't think like that. They simply couldn't get caught. He took a deep breath and exhaled. He'd have to channel some of Great-Granddad's courage and start to think like a spy.

"We have to give them multiple targets to track. We need to separate," Ellie said.

"Right," said Gavin. "But one of us has to stay with Ford. He can't be left alone."

"Agreed," said Ellie.

Ford pushed through Ellie and Gavin. "Separate? No way. That is always when things go bad in the movies. As soon as the lead characters split up, the bad guys take them out—one by one."

"I know you're scared, but we aren't in the movies. This is our best chance to try and lose them and then meet up at the café," Gavin explained.

Ford looked over at the car. *Why hadn't they gotten out? What were they up to?* Ford shook his head. "I dunno—"

"Gavin's right. It might not be ideal, but it is our best chance of ditching those two. You guys stick together. I'll go on my own. The café isn't very far from here." Ellie pulled out her phone and began typing. "Gavin, I'm sending you the café address, so you can find your way."

Ford gulped. He didn't have a better plan. "I sure hope you guys are right."

Gavin's phone pinged. "Let me just set the address into Google maps…" Gavin typed quickly, "…and… we'll be…good…to go!"

"Good. Now, on the count of three, you two head around the building to the left. I'm going to take a different route. One, two, three—RUN!"

"Waaaahhhaaahhhaaaaaaa," Ellie shrieked and sprinted straight into the parking lot, weaving between cars, heading towards the spies.

"What is she doing?" Ford said to Gavin.

"I think she is providing a distraction. Let's go, Ford."

The brothers ran. Hard. They peeled around the corner and across a stretch of grass to the front parking lot. Dodging between cars, Ford quickly outpaced Gavin, fear fueling his stride.

"Hey, wait up!" called Gavin, struggling to keep pace.

"Sorry." Ford slowed to a jog as they approached the front street.

"This—way," Gavin said, his phone held tightly in his hand, his face beet red. He looked as if he might pass out. "Follow—me." He sounded like he might pass out too.

They continued for a good 200 metres before Gavin led them down a narrow alleyway. Ford looked over his shoulder. They were alone. Memories of his dream and running from Nazis flashed in his mind. At least there weren't any Nazis chasing them. And they weren't being shot at.

"How much further?" Ford asked.

Gavin glanced at his phone. "Ten—minutes, but at this—pace,—maybe five or—six."

"Gav...can you run for another five or six minutes?"

"I—will—try."

Gavin led them onto a smaller side street crammed with shoppers and market stalls, forcing them to slow to a fast walk.

"I wonder how Ellie's doing," Ford said. "I hope we didn't make a mistake leaving her behind."

Gavin shrugged and swallowed. "Can't—really —talk."

"Right." Ford stopped walking to allow his brother a moment to catch his breath. He laughed. "I am pretty sure you need to join the gym when you get back to Winnipeg."

Gavin smiled, but it looked more like a grimace. He clutched his side. "Cramp."

Ford stifled another laugh. Gavin glared and pointed to another alley across the street. "There."

The brothers waited for a car to pass, then crossed over and ducked into the narrow alley. "You know, you are sounding more and more like a caveman. Cramp. There. Me out of shape."

"Ha—ha," Gavin said, now massaging his side.

"Me laugh. Ha—ha—ha."

Gavin grabbed Ford and wrapped his arm around Ford's neck, pinning him in a head lock. "Me—nuggie," Gavin said, grinding his knuckles into Ford's skull.

Ford twisted free as they approached another street. "Okay, okay. I'll stop."

Gavin stood tall and breathed deeply. "Not much farther," he managed to say with much less gasping. "And you're right. I am out of shape."

Ford looked back down the alley. "I think we lost them. Ellie's plan worked."

Gavin smiled. "Yup, so far, so good."

CHAPTER 20

The wind pushed Ford gently along the boulevard. Cigarette butts and litter swirled in frantic circles along the sidewalk—just like a dust devil at home.

Gavin looked at Ford and then pointed at the miniature tornado, laughing. "Are you doing that with you mind powers?"

"Ah, no" Ford laughed with him. "I can't move things with my mind. I am not a superhero, I'm just—" Ford lowered his voice. "Psychic." Saying it out loud gave him a bit of a nervous thrill.

They stopped to check Gavin's phone. "We should be close."

A hand rested on Ford's shoulder. "Gah!" He said and jumped high.

"Sorry!" Ellie said. "Didn't mean to frighten you."

"You lost them," Gavin said. "You had us worried. You kind of went all kamikaze back there."

She laughed. "Yup and it worked. They saw me coming straight for them and they just took off. Sped away so fast, they left tire marks on the pavement. I guess they don't want to be caught just as much as we don't want to be caught."

"Huh," Ford said, as they kept walking. "I guess not,

but isn't that the whole point of spying on someone? Aren't you supposed to want to catch them?"

"Maybe or maybe they are just waiting for the perfect time to pounce," Ellie said. "And it was a man and a woman, maybe the same pair Marie-Claire met."

Gavin stuffed his phone in his back pocket. "We're here."

Ellie looked across the street at *Les Deux Magots*. "It sure doesn't look like anything special. I mean it's full of history and all that, but it's exactly like every other old restaurant we've seen in Paris. Tables jam-packed along the sidewalk with all the chairs facing outward toward the street."

"Parisians like to see and be seen—it is sort of their thing," Gavin explained.

Ford smiled. "Thank you, Documentary King." He looked over his shoulder and down the street. "I can't shake this creepy feeling that we're being watched."

Gavin stared down the street, too. "I don't see anything that looks suspicious, but we should still do this as quickly as possible. I'll stay on the lookout for undercover agents and Ellie will take copious notes. You just tell us everything you see. Hopefully that will be enough."

Ellie shook her head. "No way! With Ford waving his arms around, jogging on the spot, and giving us a running commentary on what only he can see, we'll look a bunch of lunatics. We need to get a table out of the way and try to blend in with the locals."

Ford looked at the café. There were a few empty tables off to one side. "She's right. If we want to outsmart spies, we need to think like spies."

"Time to go undercover and, since we're living in an actual spy movie, we need code names." Ellie tapped her chin with one finger as she thought. "Got it! Ford, you are The Wizard, like the all-powerful Wizard of Oz, because what you do is sort of like magic and Gavin, your code name is The Professor, because you are a walking textbook."

"And what is your code name?" Ford asked.

"I have saved the best for last." Ellie stood like Superwoman with her hands on her hips and her chest puffed out. "I am...*The Mastermind!*"

Ford laughed. "Mastermind? Is that because your head is swollen from your massive ego?"

Ellie grinned. Her eyes sparkled. "Nope." She whipped her phone out from her back pocket. "It's because I keep all the critical details of our mission plotted and organized! I am the lynchpin."

Gavin laughed. "I am so glad I ditched school. This is way better than advanced neurobiology class with boring old Professor Van Hussen."

Ellie's smile vanished. "Ditched school?"

"Oh, yeah. I wasn't quite sure how to tell you about that..." Gavin and Ellie walked ahead as he filled her in on his university misadventures.

Ford followed, scanning everyone he passed for possible spies. Somewhere out there, others were watching. He could sense it, even if he couldn't see anyone. Ford's instincts weren't whispering cautious warnings. They were blazing up every nerve in his body, screaming: "Caution! Caution! Caution!" At the same time, he could feel his great-grandfather's memories pulling at him, begging him to solve his mysterious past. Ford squared his shoulders and let out a long breath.

"I'll do it for you, Great-Grandpappy," he murmured. "But this sure better be worth it."

Ford zipped in front of Ellie and Gavin. "Professor, Mastermind, follow my lead. Time for Mission Great-Granddad Mystery to begin."

Ellie smiled. "I like how you think, Wizard."

Ford led them to an empty table as far from the restaurant's entrance as possible. "This should be good." Ford sat behind the table with his back to the outside wall of the café. "You guys sit on either side of me and try to block me from view. That way, if I go nuts, no one will be able to see. And we should order in French so we don't stand out and if the secret service agents ask about English-speaking North Americans, the waiter won't think of us. Oh, and one more thing. Let's order something that doesn't take long to cook so we can eat fast and then be left alone long enough to have my vision!"

"All good ideas. Very spy-like," Ellie said. She slipped off her baseball cap and set it on the table. "I don't want to stand out and so far, I haven't seen one other girl in Paris with a cap on, let alone a very distinctive Baltimore Orioles cap." She removed her scrunchie, freeing her locks from the ponytail, and ran her hands through her long, curly, black hair, smoothing down the poof.

"I was—" Ford began, but immediately went silent as a waiter approached. He looked at Ellie's hat and smiled. Ellie grabbed it and stuffed it in her backpack.

"*Je suis désolée!*" Ellie apologized and continued in rapid-fire French. Ford couldn't understand one single word. When she finished speaking, the waiter frowned. Ford thought he might be confused, but Ellie said something about being in a hurry.

"*Ah, la jeunesse*," he said, chuckling and moving along to another table.

Gavin grinned. "You really are good at French, Ellie."

"Yeah, I couldn't follow you at all," Ford added.

Ellie beamed. "You will both be happy to know that in addition to ordering us the soup of the day, we each are getting a large *café au lait* and a piece of chocolate cake for desert. I asked him to bring everything at once, which he found pretty amusing."

"I hope we weren't too amusing. We don't want him to remember us," Ford said.

"Let's hope not," Ellie said, glancing at her phone. "It's now one o'clock. As soon as we get our food, I say you go on your blast from the past, Ford."

"Wait, wait, wait. First, I am eating my lunch. Breakfast was forever ago and I am starving."

"You are always starving."

"Yes. And your point is?"

"Ford does need to eat, Ellie. Surely we have time to eat? And I've noticed the visions sap his strength. Plus, wouldn't the waiter find it strange if we ordered a bunch of food but never ate even one bite? We would stand out in his mind. Remember, we don't want to be memorable. We want to blend in with our surroundings."

"Right. Act like a local," Ellie said. She looked at the people sitting around them. "Does anyone look suspicious to you two?"

Gavin scanned the other patrons. "Not really. They all look like normal people. Some are obviously tourists, like that family over there with the mounds of Notre Dame Cathedral shopping bags. But no one looks dark and sinister."

"Speaking of dark and sinister, I am pretty sure someone was following us yesterday too," Ford said.

"What?! When?" Ellie asked.

"When we arrived home from the library. I thought a car was following us."

Gavin frowned. "Why didn't you say something?"

"I assumed I was imagining things, but with the agents questioning Marie-Claire today and then the parking lot—"

"Now you know it wasn't simply your imagination," Ellie finished for him.

"Exactly."

"Shhh!" Gavin said, whispering. "The waiter is coming."

Gavin and Ford sat silently as steaming bowls of soup were placed in front of them. A robust mixture of tomatoes, carrots, and zucchini wafted across their table, making Ford's mouth water. He was just about to comment when he remembered. No English.

"*Merci,*" Ellie said as the waiter crammed the coffees and cakes onto the small table.

"*Bon appétit,*" he said and smiled. He tucked his tray under his arm and circulated amongst the other tables.

Ellie took a spoonful of soup. "Holy moly! This is amazing." She sipped three more spoonfuls in rapid succession. "So gooood."

Ford sliced into his chocolate cake, spearing a large wedge with his fork. He stuffed it in his mouth, crumbs falling to his plate. His eyes grew wide as he chewed. "That," he said, swallowing, "is the best cake I have ever tasted."

Gavin laughed. "Cake first? Nice."

"Why not? We have no grownups to tell us what to do."

Ellie rolled her eyes. "*Bon appétit,*" she said, in an Oscar-worthy imitation of their waiter and returned to her meal.

Ford smiled at his brother. "I see you have taken the dessert-first option as well."

"You are our fearless leader, after all."

Ford's smile grew larger. Their leader. That was a first. With every bite, he felt more up to the task.

Ellie gulped down her soup. Ford shovelled cake into his mouth.

Gavin sighed. "Pretty sure you are the first spies

in history to challenge each other to a lunch-eating contest. I have never seen James Bond speed-eat cake."

Minutes passed, the only sound filling Ford's ears was cutlery clanking on plates and slurping of *café au laits*.

"Done," Ellie said, laying her fork on her plate.

"Huh, you beat me," Ford said, nearly through his soup. "Give me a second, I'm almost done."

Ellie pulled out her phone. "I'll get ready." She then slid the creased photo of the café from the stack of Great-Granddad clues and laid it on the table next to Ford's soup bowl.

Ford's heart fluttered as he swallowed his last mouthful. He pushed down his nerves.

"All right," he said, wiping his sweaty hands on his jeans.

Time to get his spy on.

"Wait. We can't have Ford slipping into a vision surrounded by all these people, just like that," Gavin said. He slid out a tall menu that lay underneath his plate. "I think you should hide behind one of these. Pretend like you're reading it and we can be your lookout."

Ford propped up a menu in front of him. "Good idea, Gav. It can be my literal cover as I go undercover."

Gavin laughed. "Exactly."

Ellie passed Ford the photo. "Now remember, speak clearly, but not too loudly. We don't want anyone eavesdropping."

Gavin's smile quivered. "Good luck or break a leg or whatever."

The moment Ford's fingers touched the paper, his vision blurred, but the café didn't vanish like in his other visions. Rather, the café merely changed, ever so slightly. The tables crammed with tourists on iPads and phones morphed into Nazi soldiers crowded around tables brimming with coffees and pastries.

"I'm still here on the patio, but back in 1944. The place is crawling with Nazis. Not a lot of civilians in sight." Ford looked around. "There's just the waiters, a handful of men in business suits mingling with the soldiers, and a few women walking very quickly down the street."

Ford turned and looked through the café window into the restaurant. "So far, no Great-Granddad."

He sat back in his chair and watched soldiers sipping coffees, eating decadent pastries, and laughing with each other. "It's like the Germans are on some sort of holiday but it's the middle of the war." How could Nazis act so...normal?

Ford swivelled around and stared down the boulevard. A man in a tan trench coat flanked by two officers approached. "I think it's him." The men came closer. The civilian tipped his hat at the maître d'. His blue eyes flashed. "Yup, it's Great-Granddad. He's here."

The three men traipsed straight into the restaurant and out of sight. Ford leaped to his feet and dodged through the jam-packed tables, trying hard not to walk through anything or anyone.

Ford came too close to a large soldier and stepped through the man's foot. Hot pins and needles burned up his leg. "D'oh! Nazi vibes."

Ford raced through the doorway and scanned the restaurant. "There. I see him. He's at a table with a bunch of officers. The two men he arrived with are sitting down, but he is just standing there talking."

What were they saying? Ford walked closer, into earshot, but it was no use. They were speaking German.

"*Heil Hitler,*" Great-Granddad said loudly, saluting the men. He turned quickly and strode across the restaurant.

Heil Hitler? What? Stunned, Ford followed his great-grandfather, who disappeared down a set of stairs. Ford picked up his pace, not wanting to lose him. Great-Granddad entered the men's room at the bottom of the steps and Ford ran and squeezed into the bathroom before the door closed. He could still feel that soldier's aura tingling in his leg. He didn't want to add walking through a mahogany door to his uneasy sensations.

Great-Granddad looked in the two bathroom stalls. They were empty. He spun and picked up a tall, metal garbage can and placed it on an angle against the door. The lid fit tightly under the doorknob. "That'll keep out the stinking ratzis."

"We've come down to the washroom in the basement and he's blocked the door," Ford said.

Great-Granddad gripped the porcelain sink and stared into the mirror. He whispered to his own reflection. "No time for second-guessing. We only have two days. If owl is going to evade capture, contact must be made."

"He's muttering something about an owl. It doesn't make a lot of sense," Ford whispered, trying to speak so Ellie could still understand what he was saying.

Great-Granddad climbed onto the sink and reached to the top left corner of the wall panel. He pushed hard on the bottom of the inlaid square tile. A click echoed through the room as the top of the tile popped forward, revealing a hidden compartment. He pulled a package from his inside pocket and a piece of paper fell into the sink.

"Crumbs!" he said jumping to the floor. He snatched the paper from the wet sink and blotted at the water with his sleeve. "Owl should still be able to read this. At least he better be able to, otherwise…"

Ford gasped. *Owl is a person!*

Ford stepped closer to Great-Granddad and peered around his elbow to read what he was so carefully drying.

"Great-Granddad is hiding some sort of instructions behind a panel in the men's room and it's for Owl—who is a man—maybe another spy? Anyway, the note is really strange. There is a drawing of an owl, then it says 13:50 and finally inside a box there is the following: a drawing of a lady—wait," Ford paused. It looked familiar. "It's that famous painting—the Mona Lisa, and then the number 2, and after that a sun and a moon. Is it some sort of code?"

Ford stepped back as his great-grandfather folded the note in half and then half again. He began stuffing it inside the manila envelope, but stopped suddenly. He stared at the blocked bathroom door, his head cocked.

Ford stared at the door too. Was someone there, on the other side? His great-grandfather silently stepped to the door and laid his ear as close to it as possible without touching the wood.

Ford's heart raced. "There might be someone at the door," Ford whispered. "He's checking."

Ford held his breath, not wanting to make any noise, which he knew made no sense. After what felt like eternity, Great-Granddad stepped away from the door, tucked the envelope between his teeth, and leaped back onto the sink. Without delay, he stuffed the package inside the hidden compartment and pushed the panel back into place. Jumping to the floor, he raced to remove the trash can and set it back where it belonged. Taking one last glance at the hidden nook, he whispered, "I should have pulled you out earlier, Owl. Stay safe."

CHAPTER 21

As his great-grandfather left the bathroom, Ford's vision clouded. He staggered, reaching out to the sink to steady himself, but the sink quickly vanished. He lurched forward. Something cool and plastic smacked him on the forehead.

He blinked, clearing his sight completely. It was a menu. He was back. He pushed away from the table, his face ashen. Adrenaline rushed through his body.

"I need to use the washroom," he said.

Ellie dropped her menu on the table. "Are you going to be sick?" She rose from her chair. "Do you need help?"

"No, I'm good. I just need to check on something."

"I'm coming with you," Gavin said. "Just in case. Ellie, you keep a lookout."

Ellie sat back down. "You're going to look for that secret compartment, aren't you?"

Ford's mouth quivered a bit, hoping he didn't look as rattled as he felt. He needed to keep calm, draw no attention to himself. "Yeah."

"No fair. If it wasn't in the men's room I'd rock-paper-scissors you for it, Gavin."

The brothers hurried through the outside tables,

into the restaurant, and down the stairs—two at a time. Ford was following his instinct, just like Mme. Bellerose suggested. Following his gut, just like Dad suggested. He barged through the doorway and across the small washroom, looking for other customers.

"No one's in here. Hardly anything has changed since Great-Granddad was here," Ford said, glancing up at the far corner of the washroom. "I wonder if his hidey-hole is still here."

Gavin followed his gaze. "Only one way to find out." He leaned against the door. "I'll make sure we aren't interrupted and—"

"I'll check it out." Ford finished his brother's sentence. He climbed on top of the sink and reached across the wall. "This is the one." He pushed on the bottom edge just as his great-Granddad had in Ford's vision.

A half-click ground behind the wall and the tile moved forward only a fraction of an inch. As Ford pulled down on the top edge, a rusty creak echoed in the empty bathroom. Excitement filled him as he peered into the compartment. It was quickly replaced by disappointment.

"It's empty." He pushed the tile back into place and jumped to the floor. "I thought that if we were meant to see Great-Granddad put the package in here, it must be important and I really hoped the package would still be here."

"Actually Ford, it's a good sign that the compartment is empty. That means Owl got his package and it doesn't mean this memory isn't important. We still don't have a complete picture yet. We still don't know why you are seeing these memories. We can't rule this one out. We have to think like scientists and not discount anything."

Ford nodded, unable to shake an uneasy feeling. It was more than an uneasy feeling. It was worry. For Owl.

"Anyway," Gavin continued. "We better head back up. Knowing Ellie, she won't wait patiently for much longer. Last thing we need is her barging in here."

"A thirteen-year-old girl infiltrating the boy's washroom is definitely unforgettable."

Ford's stomach growled. "Man, I could eat a second lunch."

"Don't tell Ellie. She'll freak." Gavin placed his hand on the doorknob. "Race you to the top!"

He yanked the door open and Ford leapt through the doorway and into the chest of a tall, thin man in a navy suit. Sunglasses fell from the man's breast pocket and clanked onto the tiled floor. He glared at Ford, but didn't say a word.

"Oh, *pardonnez-moi!*" Ford said.

Gavin picked up the man's glasses and handed them to him. "*Je suis désolé*," Gavin said, pulling Ford past the stranger. Ford could feel the man watching them as they climbed the staircase. When they got to the top, Ford turned to look back. The man was standing at the bottom, staring up at Ford. A prickle of fear ran through him. Instinct told him to run.

"We gotta go. Now," Ford said, pushing Gavin toward the front door.

They ran to Ellie who was counting money onto the table. "Just paying the b—"

"We're being followed," Ford interrupted her, his voice a hushed whisper. He grabbed his backpack and led them through the tables of diners. "Which way to the Louvre?" he asked Ellie as they reached the sidewalk.

Ellie pulled her phone out of her pocket. "Follow me. Mastermind at the helm."

They jogged along the sidewalk for a while, dodging around pedestrians, then slowed to a hurried walk. A wave of dizziness passed over Ford. He needed to eat. He twisted his backpack around and unzipped it, searching for food.

Ellie checked her phone and pointed straight ahead. "This way. So, what happened back there?"

"We came out of the bathroom and ba-bam I ran right into this guy," Ford explained. "I think he was spying on us."

Gavin looked behind them, panting. "I—don't think—we're being followed."

"Was he thin, really tall, with blond hair?" Ellie asked. "And did he have sunglasses?"

Ford nodded, yanking a squashed bag of pretzels out of his bag. They were from the plane trip from Canada. He was so hungry he would've eaten a two-day-old tuna fish sandwich. "Yeah, in fact he dropped his sunglasses when I smashed into him."

Ford ripped open the bag and tipped pretzel crumbs into his mouth.

"That may be the same man from the library parking lot. I didn't get a very good look, but it could be the driver of the car," Ellie said, her words fading away as they approached a busy intersection. She glanced at the map on her phone. "We need to cross and walk along the Seine until we get to the *Pont des Arts* footbridge and then we're literally three minutes from the Louvre museum."

"Good," said Ford, swallowing down dry pretzel, as they darted across the *Quai Malaquais Boulevard*. He looked behind them. His arms prickled with goose-bumps. "Because I am getting that feeling I got in the library parking lot—someone is watching us."

Gavin flung his arm across his brother's chest and pushed Ford behind them. "Ellie, you bring up the rear. No one is getting to Ford."

Ellie did as instructed, never slowing. "I know you'll probably blow out your lungs, Gav, but we have to pick up the pace. If we're being watched, we need to get to the Louvre at lightning speed. And Ford, put away the food already. We just ate."

"Right. More running," Gavin said, breaking into a run. "We'll have covered half of Paris by the time we're done."

"At least you'll be in great shape by the time we're through our European adventure," Ellie said and laughed.

Ford wished he could laugh along with her, but his mind was too busy trying to figure out why these undercover agents were so focused on tracking them. Why did poking around in their great-grandfather's war records trigger an alarm? What exactly did these agencies not want them to find?

Ellie overtook Gavin as they raced across the foot-bridge and down the steps. "Follow me," she said as she ran across the street. Gavin puffed hard, but didn't slow as they darted between clumps of pedestrians. They got tangled in a group of American backpackers, but freed themselves without too much delay.

Ellie pointed to the Louvre. "There!" They slowed as the crowd thickened before them.

Ford relaxed, all tension disappeared from his shoulders. "Hey, you guys. We lost them."

Gavin wiped his forehead with his hoodie sleeve. "How do—you know?"

"Instinct. I can't sense them anymore. They just vanished when we were on the bridge."

"Huh. That was easy," Ellie said.

"Yeah, maybe too easy," Ford agreed. "How could three teenagers shake professional secret service agents off our tails, unless—" Ford came to a halt. "That's it! They aren't interested in catching us at all. All they've done so far is watch us. If we get too close to them, they back off. Like back at the library when you ran after them, Ellie and when I literally ran into that man at the restaurant."

They slowed to a crawl, forcing people to squeeze past them.

"Hey, yeah. If you ran into the arms of a spy, why didn't they detain you?" Gavin asked.

"Because they want us to continue and they want to watch our every step. Whatever we are hoping to find out, whatever secret is lost in the past, they want to know it too."

Ellie smiled. "That is it. They need us to keep running from clue to clue, so they can—"

"Find out what Great-Granddad did during the war," Gavin chimed in, then he frowned. "But, wait that doesn't make sense. Why wouldn't they know what their own spy was up to?"

"Well, we don't know which spy agencies are following us," said Ellie.

Ford stopped walking altogether. His mouth dried. A horrible thought came to mind. "Or maybe it's because Great-Granddad went rogue."

CHAPTER 22

"What? No way did he go rogue. Our great-grandfather was a hero. Just ask my mom. Or your mom," Ellie said. "I mean, he earned the Member of the British Empire medal. They don't give those to just anyone. You get it for extreme acts of courage."

"I agree with Ellie. No way did he side with the Nazis. He wasn't a traitor."

Hold on. I'm not saying he went to the dark side, I'm saying maybe he did something that wasn't in keeping with the S.O.E. or his mission or…"

"Or what?" Ellie asked.

"I don't know." Ford thought of Great-Granddad's words from the café vision. "Back there, at the restaurant, he said he should have pulled Owl out sooner. He sounded worried that Owl was in danger."

"Sounds like he was responsible for Owl's safety. I bet he was a mission leader," Ellie said.

"A mission controller—a spymaster. Maybe…" said Gavin. "Maybe that's why he got that medal."

"Sounds likely, but I still have a feeling that something else happened. Something bad," Ford said.

"Hmmm," Ellie peered through the crowd. "How about you keep thinking that over while we walk? We still have to get through all these people to actually reach the Louvre."

"So what did you guys think about that coded message he left Owl?" Ford asked as they wound their way through the tourists, inching their way closer. "What was it again, an owl and a sun and moon and… the Mona Lisa?"

Ellie whipped out her phone. "Let me see what I wrote down…" her words died away as she scrolled down her screen. "Here! You said there was an owl, then 13:50 and inside a box was a drawing of the Mona Lisa painting, then the number 2, and after that a sun and a moon."

"Okay, so now we know Owl is a spy, or at least we think he is—" Ford began.

"And 13:50 could be military time, so 1:50 pm. The Mona Lisa could be—" Gavin was then interrupted by Ellie whose words tumbled out fast.

"The Mona Lisa has always hung at the Louvre, which is our next Great-Granddad stop. He wanted us to come here."

"But what about the rest of the code?" Ford asked.

"Well, sun and moon could represent both day and night and the number two…" Ellie trailed off.

"The number two could mean two days and two nights. So, if we put it all together—"

"Owl was to meet Great-Granddad at 1:50 pm at the Louvre in two days!" Ford said, nearly yelling.

"Well done, Wizard," Ellie said.

Ford grinned. "We are a pretty good team."

Ellie pulled the Louvre postcard from her back-pack. "Might as well be ready."

They passed through an archway into a large open square. Tourists were everywhere and they needed to find someplace quiet.

"Let's get away from everyone," Ford said, leading them off to the side and closer to the building itself, where they could talk in private. When they were well out of earshot of any strangers, he pointed to the post-card. "Can you hold it up for me? I want to check something out."

Ford held his hand an inch or so from the paper. A gust of wind fluttered it, pushing it closer to his finger-tips. He yanked his hand back, narrowly avoiding making contact. Ellie held it firmly in two hands and Ford hovered once more. Déjà vu wafted from it. The paper shimmered. Ford squinted. He could barely make out a man standing by a corner of the building.

It was like a transparent veil separated them. The man turned his face. Ford gasped. Great-Granddad came into focus and he looked alarmed. Something was definitely wrong. Great-Granddad disappeared.

"We need to go through that next archway," Ford said, looking across the plaza. "Follow me."

Ford's feet fell heavily on the pavement as he darted through throngs of people to the next square. He slowed only a little as they approached the modern glass pyramid entrance. Ford wove through the wide queue waiting to get inside. Ellie kept up. Gavin was only a few steps behind. A sense of urgency mixed with dread quickened his pace until they reached the spot he had seen in his hazy vision.

"This is it?" Ellie asked.

Ford looked at the massive stone building and its tall arched window. "Yes."

Gavin stood close to Ford and scanned the busy courtyard. "Better hurry. If someone is watching us, there is no way we will find them in this massive crowd."

Ford's heartbeat quickened. With the back of his hand, he wiped beads of sweat from his forehead. There were hundreds of people here. His voice trembled as he spoke. "It could be anyone. We need to be fast."

Ellie passed Ford the postcard. The moment his fingers grasped the card, the square in front of them flickered and greyed. The pyramid faded into oblivion and the tourists milling around them blinked out of sight, first by ones, and then by twos, and finally large groups vanished altogether. Instead of families and tour groups marvelling at the sights, Nazi troops goose-stepped in formation on the other side of the plaza. Only a few civilians remained, and they walked with purpose, seemingly eager to be anywhere but here.

"Nazis are here too," Ford said, searching for their great-grandfather. "I think I see him. At least I think it's him. He's got the same hat, the same coat...yup that's him, but he's got a limp and he's walking a brown dog—I think it's a Labrador Retriever."

Had he hurt himself? And when did he get a dog? Maybe it was all part of his disguise.

"He's coming straight this—"

Ford leaped to the side, only just clearing the way for his great-grandfather. Last thing Ford wanted was another soul collision.

His great-grandfather stood for a few moments, scanning the area. His foot tapped the ground. He whapped the handle of the dog leash against his thigh. "Come on, Owl. Where are you? It's been two days," he muttered and wobbled along to the side of the building. Ford followed.

They stopped under the shade of a large tree whose branches arched wide, touching the stone walls of the museum. Great-Granddad removed his fedora, smoothed his hair back, and eased his hat back in place.

"Jacques. *Garde*," he said to the dog, who immediately stood still and alert. His ears perked forward, his tail ramrod straight. A low growl emanated from Jacques as he looked out to the open square.

"We were right about the letter. Owl was supposed to meet Great-Granddad here, but he is a no-show. Great-Granddad looks worried. Jacques—his dog—is protecting him."

His great-grandfather crouched down, partially hidden from view by the large Labrador, and leaned against the building. He pulled out a jackknife and flipped the blade open. Pushing hard into the stone, he began carving a shape.

"He's making a mark on the wall. It's—" Ford squinted. "He's carving some sort of dog, with pointy ears. No, wait. I think it's a fox. Next to it is an owl and now he's—"

Jacques growled louder. His great-grandfather stopped carving and peered around the dog's shoulder. Walking very quickly towards them and shoulder-checking like he had a twitch was Wilhelm. Great-Granddad leapt to his feet. Jacques growled louder and lunged at the German. Wilhelm jumped to the side, Jacques leapt again and pinned him to the wall, snarling.

"Wilhelm's here and I don't think Jacques likes him," Ford said. "They say dogs can sense things we can't. I wonder what he knows about Wilhelm that we don't know."

"*Non, Jacques. Couche*," Great-Granddad said, yanking on the leash. Jacques backed down, but a low growl remained.

Wilhelm stepped away from the wall and tipped his hat with a trembling hand. "*Danke.*" Wilhelm's voice shook.

Great-Granddad looked over Wilhelm's shoulder and grabbed his arm, pulling him further under the shade of the tree and out of sight.

"I have news for you and I need a favour. It's of the utmost urgency."

"*Ja*. What do you need?"

"I'm looking for one of my agents. He was supposed to meet us here. My intention was for you to get him underground, but—"

"Underground? Francis, how would I do this? Hiding your spies is not part of our agreement. That is a dangerous favour you are asking. Very dangerous."

"I do realize the risk to you and the compensation would be generous. However, my agent has gone missing."

Wilhelm's gaze flicked to the ground and back up. "That is unfortunate."

"Yes, it is. He may be in German custody. Has there been any talk of an American, late twenties, dark brown hair, fluent in French, German, and Italian?"

Wilhelm cleared his throat and shook his head. "*Nein, nein*. There has been no chatter. If I hear anything, I will tell you."

Ford watched Wilhelm's every move. So did the dog.

"Great-Granddad needs Wilhelm to find out anything he can about the whereabouts of Owl. He thinks the Nazis may have him. Wilhelm sounds nervous," Ford said, his intuition telling him that Wilhelm was lying—or at least not telling Great-Granddad everything.

Jacques growled louder and bared his teeth. Wilhelm lurched back, his face pale. Great-Granddad pulled quickly on the leash. The dog settled.

"Listen, old chap, to thank you for your last package, I have some intelligence about an air strike—an air strike on Dresden. That is where your family is living, correct?"

Wilhelm nodded.

"You need to move them. Soon."

"An air strike? On Dresden? *Nein.* It is a porcelain-making city. There is nothing of military importance there. It has never been bombed—not once."

"Wilhelm, you must believe me. My information is solid."

"It does not sound likely and how do I explain to my wife and to the authorities why I am making a second move in less than a year?"

"You are a master manipulator. Make something up. I have no reason to lie. Our agreement was that I help keep your family safe and reward you at the end of the war in exchange for information regarding any future strikes on Britain. Look how well you did providing me with the photos of the Nazi bombing maps. That saved British civilian lives."

Wilhelm nodded. "And now you have changed this agreement. You want me to poke around German Intelligence to find your missing spy. I am a lowly clerk. It is extremely dangerous to mess with the SS. Extremely."

Great-Granddad cocked his head, his eyes narrowed. "We are on the same side, aren't we Wilhelm? I know we have this façade well-constructed, but ultimately, you are striving for an Allied win, are you not?"

"*Ja, ja*, of course," Wilhelm stammered. "I was only thinking of my children. If my superiors found out..."

"Yes, I do understand, but I am sure you understand how important you are to me, to the whole war effort, in fact." Great-Granddad pulled his trench coat sleeve back and looked at his watch. "You should go. You've been here too long already."

"Farewell, Francis. And thank you for your warning. I will consider it."

"Please do, Wilhelm."

Wilhelm clicked his heels, his arm shot upwards, then he stopped abruptly, changing his obvious Nazi salute into a cough. The dog snarled again.

"Great-Granddad's watching Wilhelm leave," Ford said. "I just don't trust that man."

Great-Granddad stroked the dog's back. Jacques's growling ceased.

"So much just happened. I don't know where to start. Great-Granddad tried to warn Wilhelm that his family was in danger, but Wilhelm didn't seem to believe him. Now Wilhelm's supposed to watch out for any signs of Owl."

Great-Granddad dropped the dog leash. "*Ici, Jacques. Garde,*" he said and crouched down.

"He's back to carving on the wall. He—"

Jacques growled, his ears jerked forward. Great-Granddad shot to his feet. Ford twisted to see two Nazi officers heading towards them. Ford stepped back further under the shade of the tree.

"Not enough time," Great-Granddad said, jamming his knife into his pocket. "*D'accord, Jacques. Piste. Vite,*" he commanded the dog, letting go of the leash.

Jacques began barking and raced across the square, directly into the path of two Nazi officers.

"Let's hope those Krauts fall for it," Great-Granddad muttered and staggered out from under the tree's shade, limping after Jacques.

Ford followed, relaying everything he saw. "He's been spotted, but he's not fleeing. In fact, I think he's using the dog as some sort of diversion. Kind of like you did, Ellie, in the library parking lot."

His great-grandfather chased after the dog, his gait more of a stumbling hop than a sprint. He called all sorts of French commands, but the dog completely ignored him and bounded between the two Germans. One of the officers reached for the dog's leash, but Jacques was too fast. He barked, his tail wagging madly, and circled them.

"Jacques, Jacques," Great-Granddad called louder, but the dog simply took off towards the front street.

"*Je suis désolé,*" Great-Granddad called to the officers, hobble-running in pursuit of the dog. The Nazis looked at each other and laughed, then turned and walked back toward the entranceway.

Ford followed his great-grandfather. "He totally fooled them. We're chasing the dog out of the Louvre grounds. Now we're rushing down the street."

They continued to the end of the block. A woman in a telephone booth at the corner glanced out at the dog, a small smile flickered on her face, until her gaze rose to see Great-Granddad. Her smile vanished. She blanched. He shook his head ever so slightly and slowed to a walk. He passed her, his limp still present. Jacques now at his side.

Ford stopped and stared at the woman.

"There's a lady. She's beautiful. She looks familiar…" Ford gasped. "It's the woman I saw in the vision from the general's office. The one who'd been beaten. She's here!"

As Great-Granddad turned the corner, the scene in front of Ford: the telephone booth, the woman, the street itself flickered, the colours dimmed. Ford spun around and the world around him grew fuzzy. As the past winked out, the glass pyramid and the Louvre rushed at him, as did Ellie, Gavin, and the masses of people in the square. He staggered to the side as he adjusted to being back in the real world.

Gavin grabbed his arm to steady him. He leaned into his brother, his body heavy.

"That was…" Ford said, searching for the right word.

"Intense?" Ellie asked.

"Yeah." So many questions had been answered; Great-Granddad was definitely a spy master, Owl was definitely in danger, and the woman from the photo was definitely important. At the same time, new questions arose. With every step they took in pursuit of Great-Granddad, the more complex his mystery became.

Ellie looked at her phone. "You did great. I think I got everything down."

"And no one was watching us. At least not that I could tell," Gavin added.

Ford grabbed his stomach. "I need to eat something."

Ellie laughed. "Of course you do." She unzipped her bag. "I'm sure I have something in here. Will an apple do? It's only slightly bruised." She tossed it to Ford.

"Thanks," Ford said, rubbing it off on his hoodie. He spun the fruit around searching for a dent-free side. He took a big bite, the cool, crisp sweetness exactly what his body needed. That and sleep. He closed his eyes and chewed. If only he could take a little nap.

"Let's go see if Great-Granddad's carving is still on the building," Ellie said.

Ford's eyes popped open. Right. Nap time could wait.

Gavin looked at his watch. "We still have twenty minutes before the parents get here."

They made their way to where Ford had seen Great-Granddad waiting with Jacques. Ford crouched and examined the brickwork. His body sagged. "It's gone."

Ellie ran her fingers along the wall. "Nothing. It's like it never happened."

Ford stood, his legs wobbly, and glared at Ellie. "Are you still doubting me?"

"No, I believe you. I just really wanted to see it, to see physical proof of all of this." She waved her arms around.

"You want proof? What about me? You've seen me go into these…trances. Isn't that proof enough?" Sweat beaded around his hair line. He couldn't believe that he had been more worried that Gavin wouldn't believe him. *What was Ellie's problem?*

"Yeah, it is. Really. And that's not it. I just— you know—wanted to see what you see for myself… somehow. It's hard not being in control, not knowing exactly what is going on. I'm pretty used to knowing… everything." Ellie blushed. "That sounded really conceited, didn't it?

Knots in his neck eased. "Yeah it did." Ford laughed. "And welcome to my world. Being out of the loop isn't always so easy."

Ellie grinned. "Sorry, Cuz." She lifted three fingers in the Girl Guide salute. "I promise to believe in Ford and all the unbelievable things he sees."

Ford smiled. "Thanks. I think. Listen, our parents are going to be here soon. We need to talk about what we think happened to Owl, and who is this woman from the photo and why is she here in this vision, and where did Great-Granddad get the dog?"

"The dog part is the easiest to answer," Gavin said. "Spies often used dogs as part of their infiltration into enemy territory. Not only were they used as guard dogs, but they helped the agents appear as if they belonged in the community. You know—just a regular Joe taking his dog for a daily walk."

"How could you possible know that?" Ford asked, taking another chomp of his apple.

"I had trouble falling asleep last night, so I did a bit of research online. The gadgets they had back then were really impressive. Hidden compartments in the soles of their shoes, maps fitted into playing cards, pens with secret compartments, and instructions hidden in coded messages that allied-friendly radio stations would read over the airwaves."

Gavin was like a walking textbook. "Professor, you truly are amazing." Ford finished his apple and tossed the core in a trash can, wiping his sticky fingers on the sides of his jeans.

Ellie's fingers hovered above her phone, ready to take more notes. "And what about Owl? Do we think he's been captured?"

Ford stifled a yawn. "It sure looks that way." Ford thought about Wilhelm's reaction to his great-granddad's questions. "I don't think Great-Granddad trusts Wilhelm. I mean, he is an informant after all and how do we know he isn't a double agent? How do we know for certain where his true allegiance lies?"

"Good point. The only thing we really know for sure about Wilhelm is that the safety of his wife and kids drives his every move," said Gavin.

Ellie looked up from her phone. "And this woman that you saw. Why is she important?"

Ford's stomach pinched, and it wasn't from hunger. Instinct again. "All I know is she is important, otherwise I wouldn't have seen her in two visions now. Do you think she's a spy?"

Gavin nodded. "It is probable. Women played a larger role in the secret service than most people realize. They were some of the bravest operatives in the war."

"I wonder—" Ellie began, but she was interrupted by a familiar voice.

"Oh, kid-ooooooooos!" Mom sang to them.

Ford looked over Ellie's shoulder. "Oh no."

Gavin winced.

Ellie spun around. "You have got to be joking."

Crossing the plaza were their parents, all four stuffed into a rickshaw. The man pulling them was drenched in sweat. He cringed when mom yodelled even louder. Aunt June snapped pictures in every direction, including one of the top of her head for some bizarre reason. Uncle Jim's booming laugh bounced off the glass sides of the pyramid and echoed through the square. Dad just grinned. He looked as deranged as the rest of them. Tourists everywhere turned to stare at the freak show that was their family.

"They have gone insane," Ellie said. "For real this time."

Ford pulled his sweatshirt hood over his head, wishing for one of his great-grandfather's disguises. They still had to tour the museum.

"I thought you said for parents, they were pretty cool," Gavin said to Ford.

"You forgot the nerdy part, and I think they just tipped the balance far, far, far to the nerdy side."

CHAPTER 23

Ford stumbled across his dark room to his bed. Even though his parents seemed suspicious when he said he was too tired for dessert, he didn't care. Great-Granddad's memories had exhausted him and he had hardly made it through the Louvre. By the time they finished dinner, he could barely see straight, let alone chat for hours over chocolate eclairs. He climbed under the thick duvet, too drained to change out of his jeans and sweatshirt. With his covers up to his chin, he curled onto his side. The moment his eyes closed, he was out.

◆

He whipped open his leather case, shoving papers inside, clearing every last item from the desk.

Mustn't leave anything behind. Nothing can link me to this hotel.

He strode to the chest of drawers and scooped out his extra shirt and trousers, jamming them on top of his papers. He pushed down hard and the briefcase lock clicked into place. He checked his watch. She's late.

Switching off the desk light, he stepped to the window and pulled the curtain back a mere inch to look down to the nearly empty street. He removed a small, round mirror from his suit pocket and angled it out the window, catching a sliver of light from the lamppost below. Quickly he yanked his hand back, only allowing the curtain to remain open a crack. Peering out he waited for ten... twenty... thirty seconds. Nothing.

Where are you, Scout?

He stepped away from the window and a shadow crossed his face. He released a long-held breath. His hand trembled as he looked at his watch again.

Get it together, man. Next meeting point— tomorrow. Plan B, engaged.

Picking up his briefcase, he slipped silently to the door. He paused and looked back to the window.

Scout. Be safe.

♦

Ford's eyes flashed open. He lurched upright, his scalp drenched in sweat.

Where am I?

Morning light streamed through his curtains and fell onto his backpack that hung on his bedpost. Right. Paris. He lay back on his pillow.

Another dream of his great-grandfather. Why was Great-Granddad so worried? More importantly, who was Scout?

CHAPTER 24

"I had another dream last night," Ford said to Ellie and Gavin as they stepped off the bus. He pulled them away from their parents who stood gaping at the long row of fountains that ran all the way from the street up to the large *Palais de Chaillot* building itself. "This time Great-Granddad was waiting in a dingy hotel room for someone to meet him. Her name was Scout and she never showed up."

"Do you think she was another spy?" Gavin asked.

"I think so and something about this dream made me think of the one I had when we first arrived in Paris. The one where Nazis were chasing me. In that dream, Great-Granddad said, 'Thanks, Scout' when a light flashed from a window. Pretty sure that flash of light was a message for him. I think he was referring to the Scout from last night's dream—Scout is a person, another spy, and that's her code name, like Owl."

"I need to add your dream to my notes." Ellie whipped her phone out of her back pocket. "Is Great-Granddad's code name Francis—I mean his code name *was* Francis? This flipping between the past and present is confusing."

Gavin smiled. "Quantum physics sounds simple,

but as scientists explore the theory in greater detail, its complexity only grows."

Ford laughed. "I was just going to say that."

Gavin blushed. "Too much info again?"

"Never. What would we do without you, Professor? As Mme. Bellerose said, we're all vital to the success of Mission Great-Granddad Mystery," Ford said.

"The early bird catches the worm," Dad said, walking up behind them with Uncle Jim in tow. "And misses all the tourists at the *Palais de Chaillot*."

Ford's breath caught in his throat. Had Dad overheard them? He looked at Gavin, whose eyes were wide.

"Are you kids ready for some fun?" Uncle Jim asked, passing them each a bottle of water and a chocolate bar.

Ellie laughed. "Always, Dad."

Gavin shook his head at Ford. Ford exhaled. Their secret was safe.

Aunt June and Mom hurried over.

"Family fun time be-giiiiins," Mom trilled.

Aunt June pointed to the far end of the long fountain. "Let's gather at the top of that terrace. With the water cannons and the Eiffel Tower in the background, we'll have a perfect family photo."

"And after that, I say we take a ride on the carousel. It will be just like when we were kids," Mom added.

"This way," Gavin whispered to Ford and Ellie, leading them out of earshot of their parents, who poured over a Paris map.

Gavin tapped his chocolate bar on his leg. Ford could tell he was nervous. "How is Ford going to see

Great-Granddad's memories if we're with our parents all day? They won't just ignore him when he trances out."

"I've been thinking about that since we left the apartment this morning. Sometimes hiding in plain sight is the best option," Ellie said.

"What do you mean?" Ford asked.

"I was—" Ellie began, but was interrupted by Mom.

"Come along kid-ooooooooos!" she called, linking arms with Dad and Aunt June, who grabbed Uncle Jim before he could scoot out of reach. They strolled in a line, taking up the entire width of the paved walkway.

"Just trust me," Ellie said, as they followed their parents toward the terrace.

The moment they reached the large stone staircase, the water guns began spraying water in high cascading arcs across the fountain. Misty spray freckled their faces.

"Just look at that," Gavin said, turning to take in the display. "You know, the fountain was constructed for the Universal Exposition in 1937. In fact, there are fifty-six water cannons, with—"

"You guys," Ford interrupted Gavin's history lesson. He pointed to the park that ran along the side of the water feature. "I have this feeling we're being followed."

Ellie followed Ford's gaze. "Do you see someone in the trees?"

He squinted and cupped his hand above his eyes to block the sun. He scanned the area then shook his head. "No, but I know someone is there. I can feel it."

"Your instincts?" Ellie asked.

Ford nodded as Gavin stepped in front of him. Gavin's hands balled into tight fists. History professor, walking textbook, now bodyguard. Gavin kept surprising Ford.

"Hey, kids," Dad called from the top of the stairs. "Your mothers are getting impatient. Time to hustle."

They raced up the stairs and when they reached the top, Ford's eyes darted back to the trees. He paused. Did someone just duck under those bushes?

"Come along Ford," Mom called.

Ford drew his gaze away, as Aunt June ushered him over to where everyone was waiting, her small tripod already set up. "How lucky are we. The Eiffel Tower across the Seine as a background—talk about a dream location for a family photo. Everyone move in close. Once I say 'cheese,' I'll have five seconds to get into position. Remember to keep smiling until you hear the click. One, two, three and...cheese!" She hurried over, squeezing in next to Ellie and Uncle Jim.

With the click, Ford craned his neck to search the park.

"What's up, Fordie? You seem distracted," Dad asked, looking him straight in the eye. "Everything okay?"

"Yeah, everything's fine. Great actually. Loving Paris..." he said. Dad's gaze didn't waver. Heat rose up Ford's neck and inched across his face. Did Dad suspect something?

Keep it calm, Ford. Think like a spy. Think like Great-Granddad.

"...everything is *très bon. J'adore fromage et croissants!*"

I love cheese and croissants?! How spy-like. Just stop talking.

Dad chuckled. "*Très bon*, indeed. Listen, I've been watching you and Gavin..." he paused. Ford held his breath. Had Dad seen something? Dad pointed at Gavin and Ellie. They posed for Aunt June as if they were holding the distant Eiffel Tower in their hands. She snapped pictures lightning fast. "...and I have to say, I like what I see."

"Oh. Thanks." Ford exhaled. Close call. If Dad was watching them so intently, they needed to be way more careful.

"I know it's sappy, but having a brother, someone you can rely on, is a really special thing. If Uncle Tom were still alive..."

Dad's words trailed off and his eyes welled with tears as they always did when he spoke about his deceased older brother. Ford shuffled his feet. He never knew what to say when Dad got this way.

"Anyway, what I meant to say was look after each other. Enjoy every moment you have together, because you never know what the future holds."

"I will—we will. Don't worry, Dad. Gavin and I, we're good." Better than good actually.

Dad smiled and gave Ford's shoulder a squeeze. "*Très bon*. So very *très bon*."

CHAPTER 25

Uncle Jim and Dad bought tickets from the booth, while Aunt June and Mom scrambled on board the carousel, giggling like two eight-year-olds instead of two forty-eight-year-olds.

"This way," Ellie said, leading them to the other side of the ride. She pointed to a row of three white horses with flaring nostrils and golden reins. Ellie climbed onto the horse closest to the centre column.

Ford sat on the middle one next to her and left the horse on the outside edge for Gavin.

"Ford, as soon as the parents get settled, you need to get into your next Great-Granddad memory. Pronto," Ellie said.

Ford took a swig from his water bottle and stuffed it back in his bag. He rubbed his hands on his jeans then gripped the pole. "Even with that huge column in the middle of the carousel, I'm worried they'll still see me." His words tumbled out much faster than usual. "There are mirrors all over this thing. And Dad is so excited that Gavin and I are getting along better that he is watching our every move."

"And that's why Gavin and I are going to imitate you. If they ask us afterwards what we were doing, we'll tell them we were playing a mimicking game. We'll explain that when one of us does something strange, the others have to repeat it"—Ellie thought for a moment—"without laughing. Hah! They would totally buy it."

"Good plan, Ellie," Gavin said. "You know, the art of telling a good lie is keeping as close to the truth as possible. I saw that in a—"

"Wait. Don't tell me," Ford interrupted. "You saw it in a late-night documentary?"

Gavin shifted on his horse, his cheeks turning pink. "Well, yes."

Ford laughed. "I gotta say, Gavin. I am beginning to feel more and more thankful for your documentary obsession."

Gavin cocked his head. "Really?"

"Yeah, I'm not joking. I know I said it before, but you are full of super useful information. Having you with us is like having our own personal Google."

"Hey, you two. The ride has started," Ellie said, as the carousel begin to spin, the frayed black-and-white photo in her hand. "Time for Ford to tap into the past."

"Wait!" Gavin said. "What if Ford flaps around too much and falls off his horse? Shouldn't we strap him in, somehow?"

"Good point. Ford, take off your sweatshirt and wrap it around your middle, then tie the arms around the pole. That should work."

Ford quickly tied himself to the carousel. His horse slowly bobbed up and down as he reached for the copy of Great-Granddad's snapshot of the *Palais de Chaillot*.

The moment he grasped the photo, everything faded. The day grew darker, night descended. The carousel and its bright lights and tinny music winked out. It was like someone was playing a movie in fast forward. A bench solidified in front of Ford and 200 metres beyond that the fountain, its water cannons stilled for the evening. He looked around. Pairs of German soldiers patrolled the sidewalks throughout the garden, stopping pedestrians as they walked along. A young couple, bundled in winter coats with a baby in a pram, presented their papers. They looked nervous to Ford as they watched one of the soldiers lift up blankets and search the stroller. The baby began to cry. One of the soldiers smiled and bent low, his face hidden by the top of the pram. The mother's eyes grew wide, she moved towards the man, but her husband grabbed her arm and restrained her. Within moments they were given their papers back and the couple moved quickly away.

"It's night and I'm standing by the fountain. The place is heavily patrolled by Germans," Ford said to

Ellie and Gavin as he looked up toward the terrace. The vast building loomed in the dark. "Great-Granddad is coming this way with Jacques the Spy Dog."

Great-Granddad sat down on the bench. Jacques sat at attention by his feet. Within seconds, a blonde woman in a navy-blue dress and a small, matching blue hat approached from the opposite direction. She kept her head down, her face hidden. She sat down on the bench, leaving a few feet between her and their great-grandfather. The woman glanced at him, then looked away.

Ford gasped. "It's the woman from the Louvre!"

"Scout. You missed our last rendezvous," Great-Granddad said, his voice gruff but quiet. "I was —concerned."

"Yes, I know, but I had good reason," she replied. "I thought I was being followed that night."

"Followed? Then you shouldn't have come here. You should have left Paris immediately."

She shook her head and smiled. "Don't worry. I lost them and anyway, do you truly believe I would leave you in the lurch? You'd be lost without me."

"Taking care of me is not part of your mission. You are to infiltrate German intelligence, gather information on who their informants are, identify German spies that can be turned, find weaknesses that we can exploit, and then you are to be extracted—by me, Mission Controller. If your cover is blown, you are to follow procedure: leave me a message at one of our dead drops and hightail it back to Britain. Or, if that is impossible, Switzerland."

"I know the proper proto—"

"And furthermore, we cannot risk losing another spy network like we did in '43. Losing that number of operatives nearly decimated us."

"Fox, no one wants losses like we took with the discovery of the Physician network. Losing over 600 agents was a crippling hit, but we are purposely small, just the four of us, so we remain in good contact with each other."

Scout stood and walked casually behind the bench to stand right beside Ford. He inched away, not wanting their arms to touch. She stared into the trees.

Ford cleared his throat, eager to bring Gavin and Ellie up to speed. "First of all, the woman from the Louvre is Scout and they are arguing back and forth about their mission. Great-Granddad wants her to be more careful, and she says there are four agents in their network, so they are safe. That also means there is another spy still out there. Oh! And she called him Fox, not Francis. Maybe he has two aliases." Ford spoke said quickly, not wanting to miss any of their conversation.

Great-Granddad turned slightly, but didn't look at Scout. "Yes, but no matter our number, things don't always go according to plan, do they? Think of Jean Moulin's capture last year. If the leader of the French Resistance can be arrested, tortured, and murdered, we are all at high risk. Paris is crawling with German secret service." He sounded frustrated to Ford. "We have to take utmost care and caution, which is why we have rules and proced—"

"Fox, I can't leave. I heard something when I was at the Moulin Rouge theatre with General Carl-Heinrich von Stülpnagel. They've captured an American and they are holding him in an old Paris hotel that they are using as a prison," she stared at her hands, her fingers intertwined in front of her. "The description fit Owl."

Great-Granddad's eyes darted her way, his jaw clenched. "Then you must leave. If he has been captured, we must assume our cover—"

"I won't go. Not yet. I'm too close. The general is only here for four more nights and he's staying at the Raphael Hotel. I'm meeting him there tomorrow and it's right next door to the German headquarters. Who knows what I can find out?"

"You are walking into the lion's den."

"Aren't we all? Isn't that we're doing here?"

"Scout—*Morah*—please. "

"I can't, please don't ask me to abort our mission. You sent me in specifically to find out if von Stülpnagel is part of a plot to overthrow Hitler and I am close. Very close. There has to be a reason his name keeps surfacing. If there really is some truth to that, think of how we can use that. Fox, I took the same pledge as you, to place duty and country before my life. Don't scold me like Nanny," she said and poked him in the bicep.

He choked out a bitter laugh. "I won't send you to bed without dinner, but I will pull rank, if need be."

"No, you won't," she said, with a sad smile. "Not you."

He didn't answer straight away, instead he stared at the glittering lights of the Eiffel Tower.

"Okay, they don't agree at all on Scout sticking with the mission, but she has made contact with that German General Von what's-his-name."

Great-Granddad sighed. "No, you are right. I won't strong-arm you, but if something happens to you..."

He stood and unclipped Jacques from his leash and pulled a small rubber ball from his pocket. He threw it far towards the *Palais*. Jacques raced across the grass.

Scout sighed and returned to the bench. "We aren't at Oxford anymore, Fox. Our carefree university days are long gone."

"Sometimes I wish we could turn back time," he whispered.

"What? I never had you pegged as an idealistic daydreamer." She looked at her watch. "It's getting late. My next meeting with the general is tomorrow at seven pm. I will find where they've taken Owl and, fingers crossed, I will get the name of the agent who has double-crossed us."

Jacques returned with the ball. Great-Granddad wrestled it out of his mouth and threw it again. The retriever galloped away.

"I am bringing in Radley to tail you."

"That is not necessary and, I..." her words trailed off as she stared down at her hands. "Fox, I have doubts about him."

"About Radley? Ludicrous. He is one of ours. England born and raised. Cambridge educated, but we won't hold that against him."

"Cambridge, Oxford, you and I both know that is

no guarantee of anything. There is something about him that gives me the chills and I can't shake the feeling that he isn't all he seems. I think it's his beady little eyes. He rarely blinks. I counted once. He can go for a minute and a half between blinks."

Great-Granddad laughed. "Your suspicions of a fellow agent are based on blinking? Surely not."

She laughed and then grew quiet. "It may sound ridiculous to you, but my gut instincts have rarely been wrong, have they?"

"I can't argue with your track record. You are one of our best field agents. Speaking of suspicions, I have my own about Wilhelm Müller."

She cocked her head and walked towards him. "You vetted him like all your informants, didn't you?"

"Yes, of course."

Her eyebrows arched and she shrugged. "You've yet to be wrong, but there is always risk with an informant. Perhaps his allegiance isn't truly with us. You said he has a family to worry about, so that does increase the possibility of a double-cross. The German secret service may have threatened him."

"Or have promised him a reward once the war ends."

Jacques pranced back, the ball wedged between his teeth. Great-Granddad clipped the leash onto the dog's collar, then looked at Scout. "If you get the faintest inkling that your cover is blown, you must abandon the mission. Promise me that."

To Ford, his words sounded more like a plea than a command.

"Yes, yes, I will. I promise. I'll make my way to England." Her eyes were soft, tenderness laced her words. She stood on tiptoe and kissed Ford's great-grandfather on the cheek. "Until we meet again, dear Fox."

Ford's great-grandfather watched her walk across the grass and slip away through the cover of the trees.

"Till we meet again," he murmured. "Some sunny day."

Great-Granddad faded to grey, then drifted into mist. A white horse head solidified in his place.

Ford slumped in his carousel saddle. His mouth suddenly dry as sandpaper. "I have a really bad feeling." Ford's words croaked out, barely above a whisper. He slouched forward to rest his forehead on the cool metal pole.

"What did you say?" Ellie said, tapping him on the shoulder. "I can't hear you over the carousel music."

He yanked his water bottle out of his bag and glugged most of it down before answering. Instinct screamed at him: Scout was in danger. "Something bad is going to happen to Scout. I can sense it."

Gavin leaned towards Ford. "Like what?"

Ford shook his head. Shivers ran down his neck and across his spine. Goosebumps covered his arms. "Not sure, but I'm afraid for her. I think Great-Granddad was too. And there is a fourth agent in their network named Radley and Great-Granddad wants him to follow Scout to make sure she's safe. Scout doesn't trust Radley and Great-Granddad doesn't trust Wilhelm."

"I guess it's hard to know who to trust when you're a spy," Gavin said.

The carousel slowed to a halt and the cousins climbed off their horses. Ford's legs shook as he stepped down to the pavement. He wavered, but Gavin was there to support him.

"Thanks," Ford said and unzipped his backpack. He grabbed his chocolate bar and yanked off the wrapper. "And thank goodness for Uncle Jim."

Ellie watched him devour the sweet treat. "I packed granola bars, oranges, and more apples for you too, just in case."

He smiled. "Thanks."

"Hey, that's why I am The Mastermind, after all."

Uncle Jim's booming laugh made them turn.

"Kids!" Dad called. "Are you ready for the Eiffel Tower?"

Ford's legs wobbled again. Already? He hadn't even recovered from this vision. No way was he ready for the dreaded Eiffel Tower.

"Oh, that took me back to our childhood," Aunt June said to Mom as The Sisters walked towards them.

"Ford," Mom said, her smile fading as she neared. She grabbed his chin and turned his face side to side. "You are paler than usual. Are you feeling alright?"

Ford forced out a smile. He couldn't let them suspect anything. If Mom even had a flicker of concern, she'd join Dad in constant surveillance. "I'm fine, I just, uhm..."

"He got a little dizzy on the merry-go-round," Gavin finished for him.

Mom let Ford go and tilted her head. "Really? You've never had trouble with rides before."

"I must just be hungry. You know how it is. I'm growing, always eating. Just ask Ellie," Ford rambled on. Mom didn't release his chin. He could tell Mom wasn't fooled.

"It's true, Aunt May. He's a bottomless pit. In fact, we've taken to carrying extra rations to tide him over," Ellie said.

"Extra rations? What is this, the army?" Dad said, laughing.

Ford froze. So did Gavin. Only Ellie seemed to retain her ability to think quickly.

"Funny, Uncle Dave. We watched a documentary on World War 2 last night in my room after dinner. Some of the lingo must have stuck in my brain. Guess we shouldn't watch television right before bed, right guys?"

Dad looked from Ellie to Ford and then finally to Gavin. "All righty then. Glad we got that settled. Maybe lay off the drama, Ellie."

"Let's grab a quick bite for Ford, so he gets some colour back in his face," Mom said, pinching his cheeks.

Ford's face burned. "Mom, please."

"May," Dad said to Mom. "Let's go find a café and give the kids some space." As he led her away, he turned and winked at Ford.

Ford smiled. That was too close.

"Oh my gosh, check out my parents," Ellie said.

Ford and Gavin looked behind them. Uncle Jim was piggybacking Aunt June, who was now wearing Uncle Jim's cap on top of her own hat. The tiny French flag on top fluttered in the breeze.

Ford laughed. "*Vive la France!*"

"Long live France? Only if they don't wreck it first!" Ellie added.

CHAPTER 26

"Man, France sure knows how to make a Danish," Ford said, popping the last morsel of *pain au chocolate* pastry in his mouth and licking his fingers.

"Are you ready to take on another vision?" Gavin asked.

As much as he wanted to see the Eiffel Tower, he was dreading this next vision. "Not really. I'm still a little wobbly from the last one."

Ellie passed him an apple. "Eat this. It keeps the doctor away. Maybe it will take the Great-Granddad shakes away too."

"Couldn't hurt." Ford took a big bite.

"So why do you think Great-Granddad had two code names?" she asked.

"Maybe to safeguard the S.O.E. mission from Wilhelm. He really didn't trust him," Ford said.

"That makes sense. He'd want to keep his informant a little in the dark as to the extent of their spy network," Gavin said.

Ford wiped his mouth with the back of his hand and took a huge sip of water. "I feel better."

"You're ready for the next stop?" Ellie asked.

"As ready as I can be. Still nervous about this next memory." That was putting it lightly, but saying he was terrified out loud might make everyone scared.

"We'll be there for you. Right, Gav?"

Gavin didn't reply. He didn't even look at her as he folded his napkin into an ever-tinier square.

"Hey, Earth to planet Gavin." Ford shook his brother's shoulder. "We're ready to go."

"Oh, sorry. I was just thinking…" Gavin held up his napkin square. He then unfolded it, lines etched deep in the paper. "See how the fold marks cross each other every once in a while?"

Ford and Ellie nodded.

"I've been looking for a way that science fits into Ford's abilities, looking for a way to explain all of this. So I went back to my original explanation using a napkin. Now, if you look at the lines that go up and down as Ford and the ones that go across as Great-Granddad, you have points where the lines meet and, in the theory I am contemplating, those points are when Ford sees Great-Granddad's memories. It's as if their timelines cross, all due to their connection with each other."

"That's a pretty cool explanation," Ford said. "Well done, Professor!"

"Kid-oooooooos!" Mom sang, every customer turning their eyes to their parents. "Time to see the Eiffel Towwwww-er."

Uncle Jim beckoned them to the doorway with his hat. The small French flag, now bent in half, looked defeated. Uncle Jim, on the other hand, looked ready to take on Paris. "Y'all are slower than a Sunday afternoon."

Together they sprinted across the road and towards the Eiffel Tower. Dread washed over Ford as they walked underneath the massive metal structure. "How exactly are we going to do this next vision without the parents seeing us? I mean, won't we be stuck on some tour with them?" Ford clasped his hands together to stop them from shaking. He needed some Great-Granddad spy courage. If only he could tap into that along with the memories.

"Not necessarily," Gavin said, reading an information board outside the ticket office. "We can take the stairs to the second floor. No way are our parents going to trek up 669 steps, which is the equivalent of..." Gavin thought for a few seconds. "...fifty-six flights of stairs."

"Fifty-six flights! How are *we* going to do that?" Ellie said.

"We won't need to. We'll stop at the first floor, which is only 328 steps. That way if the parents search for us on the second floor, they won't find us."

Ellie smiled. "Clever. Maybe we should call you Mastermind."

Ford looked over at their parents. Mom, Uncle Jim, and Aunt June were busy sorting out entrance tickets, but Dad was standing off to the side. He was staring right at Ford.

"Guys," Ford said, not taking his eyes off his father. "We have a problem."

Dad marched over to them. "Something is up," he said. "Spill it."

Ford opened his mouth, but no sound came out.

Ellie stepped forward. "We didn't want to worry you, but Ford isn't feeling 100 percent."

What was she doing? Letting Dad in on their secret was not in the plan. He was cool with a lot of things, but Dad told Mom everything and she would definitely flip out. "Not feeling well? Why didn't you tell Mom when she asked? Do you have the flu?" Dad laid the back of his hand on Ford's forehead. "You aren't hot, but you are sweaty."

"I-I'm feeling sort of..." Ford stumbled over his words, trying to figure out what to say, while avoiding direct eye contact with Dad. He was almost as worried about being caught by their parents as he was by the spies.

"He hasn't felt quite himself since we arrived in Paris," Gavin explained. "I did a little research on the internet and his symptoms seem to fall under general jetlag and adjusting his circadian rhythm to the time change. Many people experience similar difficulties when travelling overseas and, coupled with a possible pubescent growth spurt, we can't truly be surprised that Ford is not his usual self."

Dad blinked. "Well, okay then. Thanks for that, Gav. Just take it a little easy."

Take it easy? Ford's hands began to perspire. How were they going to convince Dad that he could handle climbing up the Eiffel Tower?

Ellie adjusted her cap and smiled. "Actually, Uncle Dave, whenever I'm going through a growth spurt, I find it helps to do more exercise. It feels good to stretch out achy muscles, or...something."

Gavin nodded in agreement. "Same with me. The more you do, the better, which is why we are taking—"

"The stairs," Ellie finished for Gavin.

"I don't know if that's a wise idea," Dad said.

"Really, Dad. It'll be no problem, and we can always stop to rest halfway and—" Ford began.

"And we can take the elevator down if he gets tired." Gavin finished. "Don't worry, Dad. I'll take care of him. I promise."

Ford stared at his feet. If only he could tell Dad about his clairvoyance. Maybe then Dad would trust Ford could look after himself.

Dad's eyes grew teary. "I know you will. You're good boys. Both of you. And Ellie, what a cousin you are. Couldn't ask for better." He pulled a tissue from his pocket and blew his nose. "I don't know what's got into me. Maybe a touch of Ford's jetlag." He looked a bit surprised and embarrassed by his reaction.

Gavin nodded. "Probably."

"Yes, well, let me get your tickets and you can begin your climb. You kids are a whole lot braver than me."

Ford smiled. He had no idea. Once Dad was at a safe distance, Ford turned to Gavin. "Circadian rhythm coupled with a pubescent growth spurt? Did you just make that up?"

"Sort of. I just combined the two and hoped Dad

would buy it. He is a history professor after all. Science was never his specialty."

"It was brilliant," Ellie said.

Gavin blushed, a wide smile covering his face.

Ford shifted from one foot to the other. He felt like he always did right before writing a test. Impatient for it to begin, yet nervous that he wouldn't do very well. This time the impatience was the same, but he was nervous of what he would see, of what was in store for Scout.

CHAPTER 27

As they climbed the tower, their footfalls rang off the metal steps. They moved quite quickly for the first 150 stairs, but after that even Ellie had to slow down.

"151, 152, 153, 154—" Ellie counted out loud.

"Stop it, Ellie!" Ford said, his thighs burning. "We don't need you counting out the next 200 stairs."

"Stopping?" Gavin asked, breathing hard. "Break—time?" He leaned on the railing and took a swig from his water bottle. He then poured water on his head. "Hot."

"We can't wait here all day," Ellie said. She looked up. Dark clouds inched across the blue sky. "I don't think we want to be caught in a storm while Ford is in the middle of a vision."

"Can you keep going?" Ford asked Gavin.

He smiled and sipped more water. "Yes. I'll just—go slow—I'll catch—up."

Ellie began climbing. "155, 156, 157, 15—"

"Ellie!" Ford said.

"Woopsee." She laughed, then continued in a whisper. "158, 159, 160…"

Ford rolled his eyes and followed his cousin.

As they climbed higher and higher, Gavin slipped further behind. Ford's thighs and calves were on fire, but he didn't want to stop. He simply wanted to get this next memory over with.

"We're—here," Ellie said, slumping against a metal beam. "Where's Gavin?"

"Coming," Ford said, breathing hard.

If he and Ellie were tired, Gavin must be exhausted. Ford plunked onto a metal bench and pulled his hoodie off, letting the early morning breeze cool him down. He walked across the glass floor, over to the railing, and looked down. Children raced around the *Champ de Mars* greenspace while armed military personnel patrolled the grounds. No one seemed to notice their presence. Was that what it was like during the war? Did regular Parisians simply grow accustomed to armed Germans everywhere? He only saw them in visions, stuck in the past, unable to harm him, yet they still terrified him. Ford thought of those parents with their baby in the stroller. Nope. No way did the French get used to them. They must have lived in fear every single day.

Ford was about to mention this to Ellie, when Gavin clanged up the final few stairs to the platform. Ellie rushed over to his side and guided him to the bench. Gavin panted so hard, he couldn't utter a word. Ellie dug around Gavin's backpack, yanked out his water bottle, and handed it to him.

He shook his head, and titled his head back, resembling a fish out of water, and gasped for air.

"You okay?" Ford asked.

Gavin flashed a smile and gave him a thumbs-up. "Just—have—to—catch—"

"Your breath?" Ford finished for him.

Gavin nodded.

Ellie smoothed out the old Eiffel Tower post-card and flipped it over. "There is some writing in French, but it's super hard to read. Whoever wrote this certainly didn't win any awards for penmanship."

"What does it say?" Ford asked.

Ellie squinted. "Hmmm. It begins with, *My Dearest R, You would have….ad…* adored? Yes, that's it. *You would have adored the Moulin Rouge last evening. You must go. The costumes were top guill…*no that's not right. *The costumes were top quality—the highest quality…* This part is a bit smudged. *Only the…best here in Paris and the…show only runs for…four more days,*

*although tomorrow you can get the best…*sièges de théâtre *…seats in the theatre.* Now this next part is all squished together, so it's harder to read," Ellie read much slower, taking time to decipher the writing and translate into English. "*And no need to—scout for dinner, may I recommend The Hotel Raphael? The meals are—exquisite—and of course a table booked prior to seven pm is possible.*"

Ellie looked up at Ford and Gavin. "Then it's signed, *Yours, F.*"

"Scout went to the Moulin Rouge with that Nazi officer, remember?" Ford said. "General von-Strupel-whatever."

"You mean," Ellie said, flipping through the notes on her phone. "General Carl-Heinrich von Stülpnagel?"

"Yes, and Scout said he'd only be here for four more days and the postcard says the show was for only four more days."

"Right. And she was meeting the general the next day at that same hotel. Do you think that is a coincidence?"

"This is way more than a coincidence. I think there is a secret message in there," Ford said, pacing the metal floor.

Think like a spy. Think like Great-Granddad.

"When it says, 'top quality—highest quality' maybe that means someone high up in the military like the general. And the part about 'no need to scout for dinner' was telling whoever received the postcard that Scout herself was going to be at the Hotel Raphael."

"That's right, and Scout was going to meet the general at seven pm and that's on the postcard, too. And it's signed by F. Which could be either Francis or—" Ellie said.

"Or Fox," Ford finished. "What's the address on the card?"

Ellie shook her head. "I can't tell. It's been stroked through with thick black marker. It was addressed to 'R'..." Ellie said, looking at the boys.

All three said at the same time, "Radley!"

"This must be Great-Granddad's instructions for Radley to watch over Scout and make sure she's okay,"

Ford said. "Maybe I'm wrong, then. Maybe Radley will keep her safe."

Ellie turned her attention to Gavin, whose breathing had slowed. "You're looking less like you're going to have a heart attack now. Are you ready for Ford's next trip to memory-ville?"

"Yup, all set."

Ford looked around the first floor. It wasn't crammed full of tourists, thanks to Dad's "early bird catches the worm" approach to sightseeing. "Let's find someplace where we can tuck ourselves out of sight, or at least out of the way."

"Good idea. Lead on, Wizard," Ellie said, grinning.

Ford led them past the buffet-style restaurant and the gift shop to another staircase. "There really isn't any place that gives us privacy."

"Then we have to work with what we have. If we can't hide what you're doing from prying eyes, we'll have to disguise what you are actually doing," Gavin said. "Follow me." He led them around the corner and past the fancy *58 Tour Eiffel* restaurant. He walked around the next corner and over to the far wall.

"Here?" Ford asked. "There is no cover at all. It's just a bit of floor space. Anyone can see us."

"That's okay. I have a plan. Ford, you sit with your earbuds in and pretend you are playing a game on your phone. Ellie and I will do the same, but really we'll be listening to everything you say."

"Okay, I guess it's the best we can do." Ford sat with his back against the wall and Ellie and Gavin faced him. All three with carbuds in, ready to pretend they were engrossed in their phones. Ellie held out the Eiffel Tower postcard to Ford.

"Wish me luck," Ford said, and he grasped the paper.

CHAPTER 28

A loud rushing filled Ford's ears and immediately Ellie and Gavin disappeared, as if they never existed. Wilhelm flashed into perfect focus in front of him. Great-Granddad appeared by his side. They were on the Eiffel Tower.

"I'm already here. It's never happened so fast before," Ford said.

"Where is Owl?" Great-Granddad asked.

"I-I don't know," Wilhelm sputtered.

Grand-Granddad grabbed Wilhelm's collar, his knuckles whitened, and slammed him into a metal beam. Wilhelm cried out. Great-Granddad, leaned into him, further crushing the man. Wilhelm gasped, his face paling.

"Please, Francis. You must understand—"

"No, Wilhelm, you must understand. You know where Owl has been taken. I need that information."

"I cannot—"

"You must. Remember, we know the exact location of your family. We know you moved them from Dresden six days ago. We know that yesterday they played in the park across the street from your flat. And we know how careless children can be, how accidents happen. What a shame it would be if something happened to them while crossing the street for instance, or—"

"Enough! Enough. Leave my children alone. I will tell you what I know."

Great-Granddad pressed him one last time into the beam, then let go. Wilhelm stumbled to the side and reached out to the railing for support.

"Great-Granddad is roughing up Wilhelm to get information about Owl," Ford said. "Wilhelm looks like he'd rather be anywhere but here. I think something really horrible happened to Owl." A rolling nausea engulfed Ford. Part of him didn't want to know any more, wanted to run from this particular memory. Another more insistent part of him needed to know. He clenched his fists.

Wilhelm rubbed his back and winced. "It is not what you want to hear, Francis."

"Just tell me everything. Do not leave out any details."

"Owl is—he is dead."

Great-Granddad clenched his jaw. His grey eyes darkened. "When?"

"Yesterday. They were questioning him—"

"You mean torturing him."

"*Ja, ja.* Likely so."

"Where did this occur?"

"I—ah—"

Great-Granddad lunged at Wilhelm and threw him to the ground. Metal clanked and Wilhelm's boots scuffed as he tried to free himself.

"Please, Francis!"

Great-Granddad pinned Wilhelm to the floor and pressed his forearm across Wilhelm's throat. "I said do not leave out any details." His voice was a vicious whisper.

Wilhelm struggled to speak, Great-Granddad eased off.

"Owl was interrogated by the Gestapo in a hotel on the edge of the city, *Le Hotel du France*. From there, prisoners are usually sent to a POW camp," Wilhelm said.

"You mean a death camp."

Wilhelm nodded. "*Ja*. Now may I go?"

"No, Wilhelm. You may not go. I have more questions for you. And you will answer me in a more truthful manner, won't you?" He pressed down on Wilhelm's throat once more.

Ford shivered. "Owl is dead. The Germans tortured and then killed him at *Le Hotel du France*. Great-Granddad is furious."

Wilhelm squirmed under Great-Granddad's weight, nodding his head vigorously.

Ford cringed. Nausea rose up his throat. How could Great-Granddad be so violent? This was not the man he'd seen so far.

Great-Granddad pushed himself off the floor and Wilhelm rolled onto his hands and knees, coughing and swallowing. Wilhelm's legs wobbled as he stood.

"I have another operative, a woman—blonde, 5'4", mid-40s, but she appears far younger. I have concerns about her safety in the field."

Wilhelm turned his head and closed his eyes. He sighed. Slowly he opened them and stared at the floor. "Do you know how much danger you put me in? Do you not value the intelligence I have already provided?" A line of perspiration dripped from his temple and down his cheek.

"And do you not value the safety of your family? Stop stalling. Have you heard anything about my operative?"

Wilhelm stepped back, distancing himself from Ford's great-grandfather.

"You have a mole in your network. Your agent has been exposed. They will arrest her today."

Ford slumped to the side. Cool hands cradled his head.

"Ford."

Someone was talking to him—a girl.

"Are you..." a boy asked, but Ford couldn't concentrate on his words. He just wanted to sleep.

Someone shook him by the shoulders.

"Ford!"

His eyes blinked open. The world was fuzzy, like a thick fog lay over everything and everyone.

"Ellie?" Ford said, his voice barely above a whisper.

"Yeah, it's me and Gavin."

"Did you scream in my ear?"

"Yes, you freaked us out."

"Little brother, you wouldn't wake up. I was about to throw water on you, but then—"

"Ellie decided to blow out my eardrum? Good

plan." Ford sat cross-legged and leaned forward. His head pulsed in pain in time with his heartbeat. He closed his eyes and rested his head in his hands. "My head is killing me."

"Are you hungry?" Ellie asked.

"No. Yes. I don't know. I can't think straight."

"Can you stand?" Gavin asked, his voice higher pitched than normal.

"What? Stand? I can hardly see. Even talking hurts." He'd never felt this wrecked after a memory before.

"There is a security guard coming this way," Gavin whispered.

"Leave him to me," Ellie said.

Ford looked up. The guard was standing behind Ellie. His hand was on his walkie-talkie. Oh no! They'd drawn too much attention.

"Fainting is nothing to be embarrassed about. You should've told us you were scared of heights," Ellie said, raising her voice while rubbing Ford's back.

The guard shook his head and let his hand drop. He chuckled and walked away.

"Mastermind, you have the best plans," Gavin said.

"Honestly, if we were spies back in the war, we would have kicked some serious Nazi butt," Ellie said, grinning.

"No, we wouldn't have. We would've been scared out of our minds," Ford said, his voice cracking as he spoke. He shook his head, which was a mistake. "Ow."

Gavin passed Ford his own water bottle. "Back-to-back Great-Granddad memories were too much. You should at least drink some water. Dehydration is a leading cause of headache pain."

Ford smiled at his brother's endless trivial facts, but he was too tired to tease. "Thanks."

He took a few sips and his body absorbed the water as he swallowed, as if every cell was thirsty. He took a bigger gulp. The pain around his temples eased. "Can I have those oranges?"

"Of course," Ellie said, pulling three mandarin oranges from her backpack's side pocket. She quickly peeled one and tore off a few wedges.

Ford stuffed them in his mouth. Juice dripped down his chin. "This, is just what I needed." With every swallow, the tension across his skull lessoned.

"Maybe you need a baby bib," Ellie said. She passed him the rest of the fruit and began peeling another one. Gavin grabbed the third and peeled it too.

Gavin and Ellie were silent as Ford polished off all three oranges.

"Huh," said Gavin. "I guess vitamin C is not only good for colds and flus, it's good for excessive clair-voyant activity."

Ford wiped his face with his sleeve and chugged down the rest of Gavin's water. "It sure is." Then his face paled as he remembered the last words Wilhelm spoke.

"Scout. Her cover's been blown. Wilhelm said they had a mole in their network and the Nazis are after her right now—or were after her—back then, or whatever."

Gavin frowned. "A mole? Who could it be? If Owl is dead and Scout is about to be arrested, that leaves Great-Granddad and—"

"Radley! It has to be him. Scout was right not to trust him," Ford said.

"Woah," Ellie said. "That is huge. Do you think that's why you're connected to Great-Granddad? Do you think you're supposed to save Scout somehow?"

"Save her?" Ford considered the possibility. It didn't feel right. "No. We can't change the past."

"Right, sorry," Ellie said. "That wouldn't make much sense."

"It's okay, it means you're not perfect and just a mere mortal like the rest of us."

"I prefer perfection." Ellie blushed. "That sounded really snotty. Sorry. Again." Ford smiled, but there was no joy in it. Sadness rolled over him like waves on a sandy beach. He stared at the old postcard that now lay on the floor in front of him. "I think what's made all of this so painful for Great-Granddad is that Scout— Morah—was his friend. I think…" Ford's words died to a whisper. "I think whatever happened to her was Great-Granddad's fault."

CHAPTER 29

By the time they returned to the apartment, it was mid-afternoon and Ford felt more zombie than human.

Dad pushed on the front door. It creaked open. "Well, that is strange. The door wasn't closed properly."

Ford peered around Dad and into the apartment. A surge of adrenaline shot through his post-vision exhaustion.

Uncle Jim eased his way past Ford. "Y'all stay out here while we check it out. Junie, have your phone ready in case we need to call the police."

"Oh my!" Aunt June replied, digging deep into her large, bright orange purse. "I never can find that dratted thing."

Ford tugged at Gavin and Ellie, pulling them down the hallway.

"That's smart kids, take yourselves far out of the fray," Mom said. "We want you safe."

"You guys, this is super suspicious," Ford whispered. "Do you think the spies who are tailing us broke in?"

"It is a huge possibility," Gavin said.

"Do you think they bugged the place?" Ellie asked.

"No idea. Maybe," Ford said.

Ellie's eyes grew wide, as did her smile. "I sort of hope they did."

"What? Are you bonkers?" Ford asked.

"Come on. Don't you think it's kind of cool? I mean, do you know anyone else whose home has been bugged by undercover agents?"

"Bugged by undercover agents? Don't you think that's a bit of a stretch?"

"We have no idea what we're poking around in. This is getting serious. We could be uncovering long-buried state secrets without even knowing it and we could get in a lot of trouble," Gavin said.

Ellie sighed. "You two are so boring. Why can't you just love the thrill of it?"

"It is exciting—sort of—but maybe it's time we let the parents know what we've been doing," Gavin said.

Ellie glowered at Gavin. "What? No way. We can do this. Ford, what do you think?"

Ford leaned against the wall. "We can't tell them about my abilities. Remember what Mme. Bellerose said. Plus, who knows how the parents would react." They were close to solving Great-Granddad's mystery and Ford didn't want Mom's worry to shut down their mission.

"Fine, we could leave that part out," Gavin said.

"Guys, we can't give up. Think about what Scout was willing to risk. Surely we can follow the memories of a long-dead relative for a few more days. Right?" Ellie looked to Gavin and then Ford.

Gavin didn't answer.

"I guess we—" Ford began, but Ellie interrupted.

"Woohoo! I already have a plan, scaredy-cats. As soon as we get the all clear, we're going to search for signs of tampering in the apartment. Check out phones, windows, under beds, around lamps, basically everywhere." Her face was all smile and her eyes sparkled.

Ford couldn't help smiling back. "It is pointless arguing with you," he said.

"Exactly," she crossed her arms and stared at Gavin. "So, Professor. Are you in?"

"What choice do I have?"

Ellie laughed. "Absolutely none."

Dad reappeared in the apartment doorway. "Okay, family. Everything is exactly where we left it, even our passports."

Uncle Jim stood behind him. "I guess one of us didn't pull the door completely closed. We're in the big city now. Time for us to think like city slickers." His deep laugh echoed down the hallway.

"Come along kid-oooooooos! Time to get ready for dinnnnnnnnnnn-er," Mom trilled.

"Okay, Mission—" Ellie paused and smiled. She grabbed each cousin by an arm and pulled them into a tight circle. "Mission I Spy engaged. Inspect every nook and cranny of your room and remember, you are looking for signs of intrusion and surveillance equipment. Then report back to my room and we'll compare notes and move on to the rest of the apartment."

The cousins followed their parents inside and scattered to their bedrooms.

Ford stepped into his room and closed the door. Where to begin? He slowly walked across his room, examining the carpet and walls. He stepped into his closet and flipped through his shirts and pants. Would spies bug his jeans? He patted down his pants pockets. Nothing. He searched the inside pockets of his new blazer. Nada. He dipped his hands in the outside pockets. Nope.

He glanced around his room. Maybe he could use his psychic ability. He closed his eyes and took a deep breath. He held his hand out in front of him, like when he searched for déjà vu feelings in Great-Granddad's photos. With his hand outstretched, he reached towards his bedside table and probed for any odd feelings. The only thing he felt was foolish. He opened his eyes and scanned the room. Perhaps by the window? Closing his eyes once more, he took two steps and, on his third, jammed his pinky toe into the bed leg.

"Ow!" His eyes flashed open as he fell onto the bed, grasping his foot and feeling ridiculous. Of course it didn't work. Ford wasn't psychically "connected" to top-secret surveillance devices.

Had anyone even come into the apartment? Ford looked over to the corner fireplace. Although spies would be extremely careful...

He sighed and limped past his desk and examined every inch of the fireplace, running his fingers along the mantle. Nothing here either. He scanned the room. Might as well search the desk next. Ford picked up the lamp, checked the bottom, the switch, and the shade and, finding nothing, he slid open the desk drawer. Empty. He closed it halfway and stopped. Time to think like a spy. Ford got onto his knees, opened the drawer all the way, and ran his hand along the top of the cavity. Smooth wood, smooth wood, smooth wood, and his fingers grazed over a small metal disc. Was it a listening device? Carefully, he slid his fingernail under one edge and pried off the object. It plunked into the drawer. Ford held his breath and opened the drawer as far as it could go.

It was a bug. Someone was listening to him this very moment.

Ford's heartbeat pounded hard. Maybe he could fool whoever was listening in and make them think he hadn't found it, that the plunking sound wasn't the discovery of the disk, but something else like…like… like what?

Think Ford. Think.

That's it!

Maybe they would think the plunking sound was just Ford losing his temper looking for something. He grabbed some pens from the desktop and threw them in the drawer.

"Where did I put my…" Ford said, hoping he sounded frustrated. "…my…" What could he be looking for? A picture of Ellie taking notes on her phone flashed in his mind, *Aha!* "…my…phone!"

He slammed the drawer closed, yanked it open, and rummaged around, pushing the pens in every direction. As they rolled, he gingerly picked up the bug and slammed the drawer closed.

"Not there," he said loudly. "Guess it's lost."

He stared at the device in his palm. What should he do with it? Knowing people, strangers, were listening in on him was creepy and he fought hard to resist the urge to throw it to the floor and squash it under his foot.

His door opened and Ellie's face appeared. Ford jumped.

"What's taking so long?" she asked.

"I am looking for my phone."

She frowned. "I didn't think—"

"Yes, that's right, my phone," Ford interrupted Ellie as he held out his shaking hand. The bug sat right in the centre.

Ellie's mouth fell open and a tiny, "Oh," popped out. She closed the door and stepped closer, looking at it from every angle. Her eyes met Ford's and she grinned. "Too bad about your phone," she said with an exaggerated wink. "I'm sure it will turn up."

He rolled his eyes and mouthed, "What about you?"

She shook her head.

Ford carefully placed the bug on his desk and pointed to his doorway. "Let's see what Gavin's up to."

"What a great idea," Ellie said, winking again.

"Just—let's go." Ford opened the door and she raced through pumping her fists high in the air.

By how excited Ellie was, you'd think they'd won a million dollars, not discovered a listening device planted by some unidentified secret service agency. *Didn't she ever get scared?* Ford looked back into his room. He had to sleep in there, with someone listening to his every breath. He shivered. Maybe he could convince Ellie to switch rooms. He sighed. That would never work. Their parents would ask too many questions.

"Hurry up, Ford," she called from Gavin's room.

Ford closed his door. "I'm—" His words caught in his throat.

Something had clunked on the other side of the front door. He tiptoed to the peephole and looked out, half expecting an eyeball to be staring back at him. Ford could only see directly across the hall. Silently, he gripped the glass doorknob and twisted.

One, two, three!

He yanked open the door and darted into the hallway, just in time to see a man and a woman disappear down the staircase at the end of the hall. Were they the spies from the library?

CHAPTER 30

Ford stretched and slowly opened his eyes. Bright sunlight filled the room. He was on the floor of Gavin's room. His back ached, but at least he had slept.

"Hey, Little Brother," Gavin said, sliding to the end of his bed, his head hanging over the edge. "Why are you in my room?"

"I ah…didn't want to sleep in my room. I ah—"

"The bug freaked you out that much, huh?"

"Yeah. I know Ellie thinks the whole thing is a colossally exciting, real-life action-adventure movie, but I don't like being spied on."

"I guess it doesn't help that your room was the only one we found anything in either."

"Exactly. It means they're focused on me. Which is even creepier."

"That actually has me concerned."

Ford shuddered. "Me too. Do you think they know about my clairvoyance?"

"I don't know how they could. The only people besides us three who know are Mme. Bellerose and Marie-Claire. Mme. Bellerose would never tell a soul. And Marie-Claire…" Gavin trailed off.

"She wouldn't betray us." Ford said.

But what if she'd been threatened and she had no choice? An image of Great-Granddad throwing Wilhelm to the ground entered his mind. It wasn't the image of the gentle and loving man Mom always talked about. The secret service was serious business. Would they have roughed Marie-Claire up to make her talk?

Gavin's door swooshed open. Ellie stepped inside the room.

"Hey lazy bones!" she said, then fixed her eyes on Ford. "What's going on? You had a slumber party and you didn't invite me?"

Ford blushed. "No, it's—"

"Not important," Gavin interrupted. "We need to talk about today's visit to the Notre Dame Cathedral. According to The Sisters, we are going on a tour together. They want to spend more 'quality family time' with us. They were adamant about it."

Ellie sat at the end of Gavin's bed.

"How do you know that?" Ford asked.

"I heard them talking in the hall after we went to bed," Gavin said.

"You eavesdropped? Well done, Professor," Ellie said, high-fiving Gavin.

He smiled. "Thanks, but we still need to figure out how Ford is going to tap into Great-Grandfather's memory if we are stuck with our parents the entire time."

"I'm not sure, but once we get to the cathedral maybe something will come to us. I mean The Sisters are always taking breaks to eat pastries."

Gavin laughed. "No kidding. I've never seen my mom eat so many tortes and croissants in my entire life."

Ford walked over to the window and looked down to the street and the several cars parked along the curb. Were spies in any of them? He closed his eyes and thought about the agents from the library. His spine tingled. Yes. He couldn't tell exactly where, but they were down there. Waiting. For him. No way was he going to be used as an agent of evil.

"Hey Ford," Gavin said. "Did you hear us?"

Ford spun to face them. "Ah, no. Sorry."

"We were discussing the next clue. It's our second last one, so hopefully we'll get some more answers. It's the bookmark with that Bible verse: *And you shall know the truth and the truth shall set you free.*"

"Do you think it's a code—some sort of message?" Ellie asked.

"Maybe," Ford said, thinking about it. He closed his eyes, hoping he'd sense something that would help them. Nothing came to him. "I really don't know about this one. Sorry."

Ellie smiled. "We'll find out soon enough. I have faith in you. I can't deny what's happening to you. And finding that bug in your room sealed it for me. Sorry it's taken me so long to fully believe you."

"That means a lot," Ford said. He let out a slow breath. One step closer. Nervous anticipation and impatience fluttered in his stomach. "The truth shall set you free."

Great-Granddad's truth. Was that what they were searching for?

CHAPTER 31

Ford had never seen anything like the Notre Dame Cathedral. It was far older than any church in Winnipeg and it was at least twice the size of his entire school. He stared up at the arched stone ceiling and its faded murals.

"Mom and Dad are staring at you," Gavin whispered to Ford. Across the sanctuary, Mom leaned in to Dad and spoke too quietly for them to hear her words, but the determined look on her face and her crossed arms told the cousins everything they needed to know. "She is going to be watching us like a—" Gavin began, but Ford interrupted him.

"Like a spy?"

"I was going to say hawk, but spy is more appropriate."

Ellie waved a map in the air. "Mastermind to the rescue. I grabbed this from the kiosk at the entrance. Even though Notre Dame is huge, there aren't a lot of places we can hide away. Except for the crypt."

"The crypt? Geez, could that sound any more ominous?" Ford asked.

"Don't get your undies in a knot, it's now an archeological museum. Nothing to be scared about. Save your fear for our trip to the Catacombs tomorrow. Now that is going to be spine chilling," Ellie said with a ghoulish grin. She laughed and returned to her pamphlet.

"We can't just sneak away. Look at them," Ford said and smiled at his parents. Dad smiled back. Mom held her two fingers to her eyes and then pointed them at Ford. Dad watched her then mouthed "sorry" to Ford.

"They really are watching your every move," Gavin said. "At least Dad is on our side."

"Yeah, but he's under Mom's control."

"Well aren't you two a pair of Gloomy Gusses. Listen, we need to create a distraction so we can get away. The place is pretty packed, so that will help. We may have to split up too. Ford may have to do this one alone."

"What? No way. That is too dangerous. What if someone finds him? What if the undercover agents are watching us right now? What if they follow him and—" Gavin sputtered.

"Hey, Gavin," Ford interrupted. "You're kind of freaking me out."

Ellie glanced over to the sanctuary. "We have to be ready for any opportunity to separate from the parents."

Gavin's eyebrows raised and he slowly shook his head. "I guess."

Ellie shrugged. "No one said it would be easy."

"No, but the one thing we were warned about was protecting Ford. Mme. Bellerose couldn't have been clearer about that and I am not leaving my little brother to fend for himself. Not for a second. Especially not now." Gavin lowered his voice and continued. "We have solid proof that he is under surveillance. This is not the time to let down our guard. I will not let Ford do this alone. Forget it."

"Gee, Gav. Thanks," Ford said. Gavin got passionate about a lot of things, physics, math, history, but never before was that intense emotion directed at him. It felt…brotherly. This must have been how Dad and Uncle Tom had been together.

"Good points, Gavin. At least one of us will stay with Ford at all times," Ellie said. She slid her phone out of her back pocket and opened her notes. "There's something that is still bugging me. What was such a big deal about their mission? I mean, there were lots of secret missions underway during the war, so why was Great-Granddad's any different?"

Gavin nodded. "That is a valid question. The more we know, the further away we seem to be from discovering what they did that was so top secret."

Ford shrugged. "Maybe this time we'll get closer to the truth."

"It that your clairvoyance at work or is it just wishful thinking?" Ellie asked.

"A little bit of both, actually."

Gavin's gaze darted to their parents. "They're coming this way."

"Our tickets are sorted," Dad said. "Our tour begins in five minutes."

Mom stared at Ford. "Yes, we wanted to spend the whole day together. See how our boys are enjoying Europe so far. Keep an eye on you and your...growth spurts."

"Right. Great idea, Mom," said Ford. "And we're loving it here. Very...historic, wouldn't you say Gavin?"

"For sure. There are important historical buildings on every single block, and so many significant moments in history happened in Paris: the French Revolution and the storming of the Bastille prison; Napoleon's coronation; Charlemagne the Holy Roman Emperor; the building of the Eiffel Tower for the 1889 World Fair; and so many artists and writers came to find inspiration in Parisian cafés in the 1920s and 30s—Picasso, Ernest Hemingway, F. Scott Fitzgerald, Salvador Dali," Gavin looked from face to face. "I could go on..."

Mom smiled. "If only there was time. I didn't realize you had such an interest in history. Maybe if physics loses some of its appeal, you will follow in your old mom's footsteps. History is chock-full of countless secrets buried deep in the past, just waiting to be uncovered."

"Really? You'd be okay if Gavin suddenly decided he wanted to be a history teacher?" Ford asked.

She cocked her head and frowned. "Surely you know us better than that. Whatever you two boys decide to do is perfectly fine with me and your dad. As long as you are giving it your full effort and you find fulfillment, we will be happy. And to have another historian in the family...just think of the looooooooooong chats into the wee hours of the night we could have." She turned to Dad. "Let's get going. Come along, everyone. History waits for no Whitaker or MacKenzie!"

CHAPTER 32

Ford tried to pay attention to the tour guide, but he couldn't concentrate. All he could think about was Scout and her safety. Did Radley betray Scout? Did she get captured or did she flee to England or Switzerland like Great-Granddad wanted? And who exactly was Radley? As they approached the nave, Ford's attention was tugged to the enormous South Rose Windows on the other side of the church.

He pulled on Ellie's arm. "There is something over there," he looked across the church. "It's calling to me. I need to check it out."

Ellie followed Ford's gaze. "First, do the next Great-Granddad vision. I'll cover you. Take Gavin. He'll kill us both if you go alone…and take my phone. Make sure he takes lots of notes. If your parents notice you're gone, I'll tell them you guys went to the washroom."

Ellie pushed her way to the front of the tour group and stood directly behind Mom as Ford stepped quietly to Gavin's side. Ford cleared his throat, thinking that would grab his brother's attention. No response. Ford gently nudged Gavin's foot with his own. Gavin jerked and looked at Ford. He seemed surprised to see his brother so close.

"Come with me," Ford whispered as quietly as possible.

Gavin leaned in close. "What did you say?" he whispered back.

Ford's eyes grew wide and he nodded over his shoulder mouthing, "Come. With. Me," very slowly. Hopefully Gavin would get the message.

"Oh," Gavin said, a little too loudly.

Dad looked over and shushed them. Thankfully, Mom was as captivated by the guide as Gavin had been and didn't notice a thing. Aunt June had already wandered off, taking pictures of the pews and hymn books. Uncle Jim struggled to keep his eyes open. He was fighting his own personal battle with a serious case of the head bobs to see anything the cousins were up to. Perfect.

Ford inched back. Gavin followed. Dad glanced over and Ford pretended to be fascinated by the tour guide. Dad looked away and Ford let out a sigh of relief. The brothers stepped back as their tour group moved along to examine a bust of some long-dead statesman.

Gavin and Ford raced to the entranceway to the crypt and nearly tripped down the staircase. Ford led them to the furthest corner he could find, which still didn't give them much of a cover. Spotlights were everywhere, meant to draw attention to the old ruins, but it also meant there were no dark corners to hide from prying eyes.

Ford popped in his earbuds. "This will have to do." He turned his back on the milling crowds. "Let's pretend we're geeking out on history."

"Good idea," Gavin said, doing the same. He held the bookmark out to Ford.

"Then you will know the truth and the truth shall set you free," Ford read Great-Granddad's writing. "Let's hope so and quickly."

The moment Ford grasped the paper, the room around him paled. "The crypt is fading away and now..." Ford paused to see what replaced the crumbling ruins. "...I'm back in the cathedral upstairs, on the other side of the church from where we just were. It's the spot that called to me when we first entered the cathedral. So far, I'm the only one here."

It was dark in the church; no sunshine glowed through the stained-glass windows. Sparse candlelight sent spooky shadows across the pews and down the aisles. Hurried footsteps came rushing towards Ford. He spun, but moved too late. Great-Granddad barrelled through him. Bright light filled him, blinding Ford as ripples of heat raced outwards from his chest and across his body in every direction.

"Great-Granddad," Ford said, choking out his words. "Another soul collision."

As the light receded, he could see his great-grandfather kneeling by a floor grate directly underneath a stained-glass window of an apostle. He took a small, metal crow bar from inside his trench coat and pried open the grate. Ford ran to his side and knelt next to him.

"Scout, this is your last chance to get out," he murmured as he stuffed a Swiss passport and a wad of money into a medium-sized manila envelope. A small fox head was sketched in the top right-hand corner.

"He has a package for Scout—money and a passport—and he's tucking it under the floor, through the grate opening. It's so dark in here, I can't see exactly what he's doing."

Great-Granddad replaced the grate. He kissed his fingers then pressed them to the brass. "Safe travels, my friend." He stood, straightened his tie and hat, and then without further pause, hurried down the aisle and out of the church.

The pews, tapestries, monuments, and smoky candles faded away. The crypt reappeared.

Ford yanked out his earbuds and stared at Gavin. They needed that grate open. Now. "What are the chances Ellie has a crowbar in that backpack of hers?"

CHAPTER 33

"A crowbar?" Ellie asked, her voice a bit too loud. Aunt June turned and gave them the hairy eyeball.

Ford opened a pack of gummy fruit snacks and dumped the entire contents into his mouth. As he swallowed, the nausea from his vision receded.

"Are you kidding?" Ellie whispered to Ford.

"Afraid not. We need one, or at least something we could use as one. Great-Granddad hid a package for Scout in this building and it's hidden under a floor grate. I—we need to see if the envelope is still there."

Ellie carefully twisted her backpack around, her gaze locked on the backs of the adults. When they didn't turn, she slowly unzipped her bag. "Let me see…"

After a few long seconds, she passed Ford an umbrella, followed by a pair of black-handled scissors. She shrugged and whispered, "That's all I have."

Ford nodded. They were better than nothing. He and Gavin snuck through the other tourists and raced to Great-Granddad's hiding spot.

He kneeled down and opened the scissors into a "V" and slipped one blade under the lip of the brass grate. He pushed down on the handle, the blade pushed up and the grate moved a fraction of an inch.

"Almost…" Ford murmured.

"What if we work together?" Gavin asked.

"Good idea."

Gavin held onto the handle of the umbrella and stuck its tip through the grate near the edge of the stone floor. He twisted it up and lifted. The umbrella creaked. The grate remained in place. He withdrew the umbrella and flipped it around. He shoved the handle through the rungs and pushed down, using it like a lever.

"Now you use the scissors and—" but Gavin didn't continue as the umbrella popped out, a metal ringing echoing around them as the umbrella sprung backwards and clipped him on the chin. "Ow!"

"Shhh!!" Ford said. "You're too loud."

"Gee, thanks for your concern."

"I think we need to ditch the umbrella before someone gets hurt. I have an idea. Get ready to pull up as soon as I jimmy the grate up a bit more."

Gavin poked his fingers into the grate and gripped so hard his knuckles whitened. Ford fit the scissor blade under the rim again and pushed down. Once more, it only moved a millimetre. He moved around to the other side and pushed. Over and over he tried.

Ford stared into the dark vent. "This is pointless."

"Don't give up, Ford," Gavin said.

Ford moved to a corner and inserted the scissors as he had already, countless times. He pushed down with all his might and the grate lifted a good inch this time. Gavin yanked hard and the grate scraped over to the side. Ford reached into the hole, his fingers gliding over the wooden underbelly of the floor, over a ridge, until he bumped into something metal. He withdrew his hand and peered inside. Too dark. Ford turned his phone on and used the screen glare as a flashlight. There, within arm's reach, was a compartment fitted to the underside of the floor and on the edge of it was an old metal clasp. He flipped it open and a long door flopped open. Ford reached inside, expecting to find it empty. Instead, his fingers found paper.

Ford pulled out the manila envelope that he had seen in Great-Granddad's vision.

"It's still here?" Gavin said. "That means—"

"Scout never made it here." Ford slumped against the end of a pew and opened the envelope while Gavin silently moved the grate back into place. "Here's the passport." Ford opened it to the photo. "It's her picture, but with a Swiss name—Ingrid Bussinger. I guess that was to be her alias."

Gavin picked up the envelope and pulled out a bundle of cash. "German and French currency, for safe passage to Switzerland."

Ford nodded. "My guess is the passport was to disguise her nationality. But she didn't make it."

"You can't know that for sure. Just because she didn't pick up this envelope doesn't mean she didn't find another way out."

The passport fell from Ford's hands to the floor. "She didn't. I can feel it, Gav." Ford tapped his chest. "In here."

Gavin stood and helped Ford to his feet. Slowly they walked through the church and joined their group, squeezing in front of a couple from Australia who were bickering over where to go for lunch. They inched around the other tourists to the front and stood a foot or so to the left of Ellie.

Ford coughed and Ellie looked his way, raising her eyebrows when she saw him as if to ask, "Well? What did you find out?"

Ford shook his head and mouthed, "Bad news."

As their party moved along to examine *Les Grand Mays* series of paintings, the cousins let other tourists squeeze in front to take pictures. Their parents seemed enraptured by the guide's thorough explanation of each painting's depiction of the lives of the Apostles. The cousins moved to the back of the group.

Ford patted the rectangular shape outlined in his hoodie pocket. "Scout never picked up Great-Granddad's package. He had left her money and a fake passport."

"We think she was supposed to use it to get safely back to England disguised as a Swiss citizen," Gavin said.

"But it's still here, which means what?" Ellie asked.

Ford stuffed his hands in his back pockets. "I think the SS got her."

"And I told Ford we have no proof of that."

"That doesn't change my gut feeling. My instincts tell me the reason Scout didn't pick it up is bad. Really bad."

Ellie patted him on the back. "Your instincts have

never been wrong. Gav, I trust Ford. If he says Scout was arrested, that's good enough for me."

Gavin nodded.

Ford flipped the bookmark over and read the Bible verse out loud. *"Then you shall know the truth and the truth shall set you free.'* The truth is Scout didn't just get arrested—she wasn't set free at all." His voice was quiet. "I think, no—I know it. They killed her."

CHAPTER 34

The rest of the tour was a blur to Ford. In a daze, he followed along until the tour guide finally came to the end of his wealth of Notre Dame Cathedral knowledge. The only word Ford heard clearly was the man's "*Merci*" and then a round of applause. The clapping awoke him from his fog.

"Are you okay?" Ellie asked as they strolled through the graveyard while their parents surrounded the guide to bombard him with more questions.

"It's like you've been in some sort of trance—not a vision-type trance, but something else. You're weren't really with us," Gavin said.

"Yeah, sorry. I've been thinking about Great-Granddad and Scout and Owl. Can you imagine how Great-Granddad must have felt? He lost both his agents. And Scout was his friend."

Ellie kicked a pine cone across the grass. "It doesn't seem fair, does it? The war ended in 1945 and all this happened at the beginning of '44. They were so close to making it. I feel so badly for all of them."

"That's the point though, isn't it?" Gavin said. "It was because of the sacrifice of men and women like Owl and Scout that we won the war. And who knows how many people returned, like Great-Granddad, changed in ways we may never understand, carrying painful secrets with them for the rest of their lives."

"But we still don't know why their mission was so important, do we? Lots of people sacrificed their lives, but not everyone had their service records sealed, like Great-Granddad did," Ellie said.

"We still have to visit the catacombs tomorrow," said Gavin. "Maybe we'll find our answers there."

"True. What do you think Ford?" Ellie pulled the old pamphlet from her bag and held it out to him. "Are you getting any messages from this?"

Chills raced up his spine.

"Yes," he whispered.

CHAPTER 35

Ford peered out Gavin's window, down to the street below. "They're out there again. Those spies. Watching us. Why don't they arrest us or something? What are they waiting for?"

"Who knows, but they can't just arrest us if we haven't broken any laws," Gavin said as Ford paced the room. "And you were probably right when we were at the Louvre. For whatever reason, they need us to follow Great-Granddad's clues. Ford, you need to get some sleep. The visions are wiping you out and the parents are really getting concerned by your appearance. You're growing paler after each one."

"Fine." Ford lay down and plumped his pillow.

"I could take the floor tonight," offered Gavin.

"One more night on your bedroom floor isn't going to kill me. And anyway, I'm so tired I could sleep on a bed of nails."

Gavin laughed. "Okay, but if you change your mind in the middle of the night, just wake me up and we can switch."

"Thanks. G'nite, Gavin."

"G'nite, Little Brother."

Ford shut his eyes and thought through the day.

Great-Granddad's words from the cathedral memory filled his mind. *"Safe travels, my friend."* What must it feel like to fear for someone else like that? To be responsible for someone's life? Ford shuddered. Poor Great-Granddad. He was a tortured soul. And that Bible verse, *And then you shall know the truth and the truth shall set you free*. What truth? And set you free from what? More questions to ponder.

He sighed, breathing deeper, as the lull of sleep pulled at his conscious mind. He couldn't focus his thoughts. Tomorrow. He yawned. He'd figure it out tomorrow...

♦

With Jacques at his side, he walked swiftly across the street towards the Catacombs. A wooden box was wedged tightly under his arm, hidden beneath his trench coat. He slowed as he neared the entranceway. The French Resistance had set up their network inside and he had to get through the maze of tombs and burial chambers without being seen. There could be traitors anywhere, even within the French Resistance. He shifted the box under his arm. It wouldn't be easy, but he had little choice. Radley's betrayal had shaken him. There was no one left in Paris he trusted and if the Nazis caught him with this, the lives of dozens of agents and crucial missions could be compromised. He could lose more than Scout and Owl. If this box got into the enemy's hands, he could jeopardize networks that the Crown had established not just during the war, but in some cases for decades.

He glanced over his shoulder. A car rounded the corner. He frowned and crouched next to Jacques, fiddling with the dog's collar.

Had his cover been blown?

Gritting his teeth, he watched the car race past him and out of sight.

No time to waste.

Nearly sprinting, he entered the Catacombs.

CHAPTER 36

Ford stared up the street to the entrance of the Catacombs. "I had another dream about Great-Granddad last night," he said to Ellie and Gavin. "He was here and he was carrying a wooden box. He was worried the Nazis would find it—and he knew Radley had betrayed them. Wilhelm wasn't the mole after all."

"What was inside the box?" Ellie asked.

"No idea. My dream ended when he entered the tombs. But the box is why we're here. I'm certain of that."

The cousins followed closely behind their parents, who were chatting excitedly amongst themselves. Mom led the pack, nearly dragging her sister by the elbow to the ticket booth. What would she say if she knew what they did about her Grandfather? Would she be thrilled to hear of his secret-agent status or appalled by how brutally he had attacked Wilhelm? What else was Great-Granddad capable of? Ford frowned. Maybe his mom and Aunt June didn't need to know what they found out.

"How do we want to handle this one?" Ellie asked, Great-Granddad's frayed Catacombs pamphlet in her hand.

"It's not likely the tour will take us where we need to go, so we're going to need to break away from the rest of the group and search the passageways on our own," Ford said.

Gavin shook his head. "That is a seriously dangerous idea. The catacombs are immense. Over six million people are buried here and there are close to 200 miles of caves and tunnels. Some routes have never been mapped. People have taken a wrong turn, gotten lost, and have never been found."

Ford fought off a chill. "I don't want to get lost in a graveyard with millions of dead people any more than you do, but we have to find Great-Granddad's box. It's the missing piece to the puzzle."

Gavin pursed his lips. "I don't like it, but if there is no other choice…"

"And this time we are sticking together," Ellie said. "We need all of us working as a team."

"Agreed," said Gavin.

"Plus, it's no fair you two having all the fun!" She forced a smile on her face. It trembled and failed.

"Kidoooooos!" Mom called, beckoning them over with a wide swoop of her arm. "We're starting now."

As they stepped into the catacombs, the light dimmed and the air grew cooler. Moldy damp filled Ford's nostrils and caused him to sneeze. A flood of déjà vu crashed into him, making him stumble sideways into Ellie.

"Careful," she whispered. "Don't draw any unwanted attention."

The tour guide cleared her throat. "Please, patrons. We have a few rules to review with you before we begin. For your safety, we insist you stay with our group," she instructed as they entered a large antechamber. "We have yet to lose anyone to the maze of the catacombs; however it has happened many, many years ago and not everyone who was lost was found—alive."

Ford gulped as they slowly walked down the first passageway. Wave after wave of nausea churned in his stomach. He clenched his teeth, willing himself not to be sick. He slowed and moved to the side, his hand grazing something damp and smooth. A skull! He pulled his hand away, wiping it furiously on his jeans.

"Ford, are you okay?" Gavin whispered in his ear. Ford leaped straight upwards. Ellie peered at him in the dim light.

"It's just, there are so many dead people down here. I can feel them," he said, his voice quivering.

"All of them?" Gavin asked.

Ford closed his eyes and focused on the swirling visions. Men, women, and children's memories circled him. "Not all of them, but lots of them. It's different than with Great-Granddad, but I can still sense their presence." He gulped, opened his eyes, and continued. "Not everyone down here died of natural causes."

A line of sweat laced Ford's top lip. He wiped it away with a shaky hand. He didn't want to be down here any longer than necessary. They needed to get in and get out fast.

Ellie stepped directly in front of Ford. "Don't let

your nerves take over. You can do this. Remember what Mme. Bellerose taught you and remember what she said. You have to have a connection to see someone's past and you aren't connected to anyone but Great-Granddad right now. You don't need to worry about anything else. Try to push everything else you are sensing away. And Mme. Bellerose also said you are going to do great things. So you need to believe in yourself. And we've got your back, right Gav?"

"Right! And remember to trust your instincts," Gavin added.

"That's right. And what are those instincts telling you right now?" Ellie asked.

"That I should run a million miles in the other direction." A lame Uncle Jim joke. No one laughed.

They slowed their pace even more so they soon fell to the tail end of the group. Their parents were closer to the front.

"As soon as we can, let's sneak away," Ellie said quietly, so only Ford and Gavin could hear.

They walked a few paces along a skull-lined tunnel and gathered around a large, round fountain filled with nothing but dust—dust from decaying bones. A full-body shiver trembled through Ford. He closed his eyes and took a few deep breaths. Ellie pulled on Ford's sleeve. His eyes popped open. The group was moving. Ellie nodded to a darkened corridor that branched off at a slight angle from the well-lit path the group was following. Quietly, the cousins tiptoed along the edge of the skull-walled room, slinking down the corridor.

It grew darker with every step. They ducked around the first corner they came to and stopped. Ford could only just make out the shape of Gavin and Ellie next to him. He placed his hand on his pounding heart, hoping to mute the thudding he was sure would give them away.

Gavin slid his phone from his pocket and turned it on. The glare momentarily blinded them.

"Let's creep back, so we start right where Great-Granddad entered the catacombs in my vision," Ford said. "Then as I relay to you where he goes, we need to follow so we can find the box."

"How is that going to work, if you're trapped in a trance?" Gavin asked.

"We'll have to guide him. Nudge him along," Ellie said, nodding her head as if to convince herself. "It should work, in theory."

Gavin's eyes bulged. He looked ghoulish in the phone's glow. "Nudge him along? Really? Does that sound like a good plan? We have never tried to move Ford during one of his visions and you really think the best place to test out this theory of yours is in a maze of pitch-black tombs?"

"Gavin, it's the best plan we have. We don't have time to waste. The moment our parents notice our absence, they will send out a search party," Ellie explained.

Gavin crossed his arms. "I don't like it, and the second things start to go wrong, I am waking Ford up."

Ford sighed. "Gavin—"

"No. That is nonnegotiable. Otherwise I pull the pin on this now. I am dead serious."

Ford smiled. "Okay, Gav. We'll do it your way."

As quietly as possible they returned to the entranceway, stopping out of sight of the next group of tourists.

Ellie held the pamphlet so they could all see it and looked at Ford. "Ready when you are."

Ford let out a long breath of air and closed his eyes. He hovered his hand above it. Dancing in his mind was the déjà vu feeling that came with every clairvoyant memory. Ford clasped the paper and out of the pitch black emerged the fountain room, but darker than it was on the tour. Ford squinted into the eerie gloom as a figure of a man appeared before him. Great-Granddad. He stood stock-still, staring over Ford's left shoulder.

Ford held his breath and slowly turned to see what his great-grandfather was looking at, half expecting the Nazi Gestapo to be standing right behind him. Ford sighed with relief. Only a dark passageway stared back.

Great-Granddad sighed too and began fiddling with a silver flashlight. He thumped it on his thigh and the light blinked on. He shielded the light with his other hand.

"Last thing I need is to alert the French Resistance of my presence," he mumbled. "And I mustn't get lost," he muttered as he hastened down the corridor the cousins had first hidden in.

Ford cleared his throat. "We need to run down the passageway the three of us just hid down. He is concerned about running into French freedom fighters."

Ford stumbled along, only vaguely aware of a set of hands pulling on his own. Within moments, they came to another passageway.

"Left, right, left, left, right," Great-Granddad said, barely slowing as he veered left down a narrower path.

"Left turn. Now!" Ford cried out. His body jerked left.

They hadn't gone more than thirty feet when Great-Granddad took another turn.

"Right!" Ford instructed.

This passageway was lined with molding green skulls. Ford shuddered as he passed a section of arm bones that had been crisscrossed in an intricate pattern. Who would do that? He kept his arms close to his sides, not wanting to touch anything in here. Who knew what kind of sickening sensations they would release?

"Left again," Great-Granddad said, adjusting the box under his arm.

Ford repeated the turn to Ellie and Gavin.

Fifteen paces and another turn.

"Left," Ford said and gasped.

The corridor in front of them was so narrow, Great-Granddad only just squeezed through. Then he and the flashlight dimmed. Shivers ran through Ford's body. Even in a vision, he had no desire to be left alone in here. Ford steeled himself and followed his great-grandfather, his back pressed hard into a row of skulls. Icy tendrils spread across his shoulder blades like a spider's web. He clenched his teeth as Ellie and Gavin's hands nudged him along.

Once through, the sickening feelings left him. "Whatever we do down here," Ford said, racing after Great-Granddad. "Do not let me touch any of the bones."

His great-grandfather slowed as he approached a fork in the tunnel. "Left, right, left, left, right. This is it, then…" his words trailed off as he marched into the darkness, the glow from his flashlight guiding his path.

"Our last turn. Take a right," Ford said.

Surprisingly, this passageway widened the further they trudged, finally opening into a round room. On the far wall, someone had carved an alcove into the stone and placed in it a stone shrine of a castle. Without hesitation, Great-Granddad strode to it, stepping over the carved structure to stand behind it. He rested the box on top of the castle as he crouched and wiggled three skulls that were stacked on top of each other in the wall.

"He pulled out three skulls behind the shrine. I think he's going to hide his package behind them," Ford said as he watched his great-grandfather pull a folded paper from his pocket. He opened the box and laid it inside.

"I may have failed Morah and Tom, but I will not allow one more agent to be taken on my watch," he said and pushed the box into the compartment. It scraped along the edges, nearly getting stuck, but he jammed it in and then replaced the skulls.

He stepped over the tiny monument into the centre of the room. His removed his fedora and bowed his head. "May God keep you safe," he paused and then, in a tearful whisper, continued. "Morah, Tom—I hope you can forgive me."

He replaced his hat and disappeared. Ford blinked. Gavin now stood before him.

"We did it," Gavin said. "I doubted you, but you were right."

Ford's eyes rolled back in his head as he slumped forward into his brother's arms.

CHAPTER 37

Ford shifted. His elbow scraped along something hard. He opened his eyes. A pair of brown eyes stared back. He was on the cold Catacomb floor, with his head resting in Ellie's lap.

"Ford, you scared us," Ellie said, straightening up. She looked back over her shoulder. "Gavin, he's awake."

Ford lifted his head. It pounded in time with his heart beat. "What—what happened?"

Gavin crouched next to him, his brows knit. "You passed out. You're lucky I caught you or you would have smashed your head."

Ford struggled to sit up. The room circled in front of him. If he wasn't careful, he would pass out again. He rested his head in his hands.

"Food?" Ellie asked.

Ford nodded, which set off a pulsing pain from his temple that raced across the side of his head and down his neck. Ellie passed him a mandarin orange. He tore the peel from the flesh and stuffed an entire half in his mouth. He chewed feverishly.

Without a word, Gavin passed him a water bottle. Ford glugged, water spilling from the corners of his mouth. The pulsing in his skull eased. He popped in the final few orange pieces and looked around the room and stopped mid-chew. His heart raced.

"The box! Did you get the box?"

Ellie jumped up. "It's right here." She dragged it along the floor to rest in front of Ford.

Ford swallowed and wiped orange juice from his fingers on his jeans. "It's really here. Great-Granddad's secrets. Right here." Ford's voice was whisper quiet. 'XX' was carved into the top. He pointed to it. "What do you think that means?"

"No idea," Gavin said. "Just open it. We want you to tell us what your gut instincts say before we tell you our thoughts."

Ford opened the box. A musty smell wafted out, reminding him of the old books they flipped through at the Ste. Geneviève Library. A tattered, leather-bound journal, old passports, a few rolled maps, and stacks of bills in all sorts of currencies lay inside.

"This was all Great-Granddad's." He picked up the journal and opened it to the first page. He looked to Ellie and then to Gavin. "Is this a list of code names for secret agents?"

"That's what we think. We'd have to verify it somehow," Gavin said. "And the list is meaningless if we don't know who they actually are or which countries they work for."

Ford paged through the book. Code names were recorded in sprawling black pen. He searched for Owl and Scout, finding their entries two pages in. Under their name was Radley. The traitor.

"So this is what Great-Granddad didn't want anyone to find?" Ford asked.

Ellie passed Ford a small black metal tube. It had a spike at one end. "We found negatives inside."

"Negatives?"

Gavin smiled. "Undeveloped photos. They were wrapped in a French bill that had some sort of coded message written on it. When we get back to London we can—"

"Okay kids," a deep, English-accented voice boomed out from behind them. "We'll take it from here."

Ford dropped the tube into the box and, as the two security guards stepped close, he threw himself over the wooden box, closing the lid with his body. He gripped the sides so tightly, he thought he might leave impressions of his fingers in the cool wood.

"No!" he cried.

"Don't make this harder than necessary," said the female guard. She sounded American. She held a long, silver flashlight like a truncheon. She smiled and Ford thought she looked eager to use it.

"Wait… you're not French," said Ellie, stepping in front of Ford. Gavin stood next to her and together they made a wall in front of Ford.

Gavin jabbed a finger at the male guard. "It's you! You're the guy from the restaurant and you've been chasing us all over Paris. What are you? CIA or MI6?"

"Very clever. I think we can leave that to you to figure out," the thin blond man said in a posh English accent. He clenched his hands, as if he was ready for a fight. "It's time you children stop playing games and give us what we've come for."

"We're not children," Ellie said. "And how dare—"

The woman rushed Ellie, the flashlight held high. Ellie's arms flew up in front of her face. Gavin lunged at the woman. She grabbed Gavin's arm and yanked it behind his back. Gavin cried out.

"Stop!" Ford shouted, as he stood on shaky legs. "Don't hurt them. Take the box."

The American agent released his brother as the English spy stepped toward Ford.

"No! Ford, don't—" Gavin said, his plea silenced as the man grabbed Great-Granddad's box.

Gavin stared at his brother. "Why'd you just give it to them? We came so far. We were so close."

"I'm sorry Gavin, but I couldn't risk you and Ellie. I just couldn't—"

"Okay, children," the woman said, drawing out the word and making it sound like an insult. "Enough chit-chat. Time to get moving."

Ellie crossed her arms and glared at the spies. "We're not going anywhere with you. If we leave with you two, you'll murder us and dump our bodies down some dark, unexplored passageway. We'll disappear without a trace."

The woman glowered at Ellie. "We are secret service. We do not murder children," she grabbed Ellie by the arm. "At least not yet. Never needed to, but keep it up and we might find a reason…"

"Okay, that's enough," the English spy said as he zipped all Great-Granddad's secrets into a black duffel bag. "We don't need to scare them to death."

"You spoil all my fun," the woman muttered, pushing Ellie towards the adjoining passageway. "Get walking and don't get any smart ideas about escaping. I'm not as fond of rules and regulations as my partner. Sometimes accidents happen in the field."

"You're CIA—you can't harm a fellow American," Ellie said.

"True, but your cousins are Canadian, which makes them fair game."

"Ellie," Ford said, "Just do as they say. Please."

Ellie's shoulders sagged. "Fine."

They followed the dim light from the American spy's flashlight as they walked single file through the passageways. The English agent brought up the rear, making escape impossible.

Ford tapped Ellie on the shoulder. "I'm sorry Ellie, but I couldn't let them hurt you guys."

"It's just—you didn't even put up a fight."

Ford slumped. "I know, but I thought of Great-Granddad and how he failed Scout and Owl and I just couldn't do the same with you and Gavin." A lump in the pit of his stomach gnawed at him. He may have saved Ellie and Gavin, but he failed to solve Mission Great-Granddad Mystery.

Ellie looked back over her shoulder and whispered. "Well, all hope isn't lo—"

"No talking," the English spy said. "Save your words for your parents."

"What? Our parents? Won't that blow your cover?" Ford asked, suddenly more afraid of the wrath of The Sisters than the two international spies.

The man laughed. "Dear boy, in these uniforms, we will appear to your parents as two members of the Catacomb security detail, patrolling the maze looking for foolish tourists who have gotten themselves lost. It does happen from time to time."

"You mean, you aren't going to arrest us?" Gavin asked.

"Or torture us?" Ellie added.

"As much as it would give me great pleasure, no. You are kids, playing at mystery games," the female spy said.

"We are not playing games—" Ellie began.

"You are either the most stubborn or the most stupid girl. I can't tell which. Listen to what I am saying," she said speaking slowly. "You are kids, playing at mystery games. A game that is now over. You will not continue your search into Edward Hugh Crawford's past. You will not poke your noses where they do not belong. You will not discuss either of us with your parents. You will get on your flight tomorrow to London and continue your European family adventure with no further incidents."

"And if we don't stop?"

The American spy shone her flashlight directly into Ellie's face. Ellie shut her eyes and turned her head.

"Are you really so naïve? Do you recall the computer issues you encountered at the library? You do under-stand that wasn't a coincidence, don't you?"

Ellie nodded. Her eyes remained shut. Ford gulped.

"We will be watching you. Remember that. We will always be watching you."

CHAPTER 38

Mom raced towards them. Dad, Uncle Jim, and Aunt June were close behind.

"Where have you been!" Mom shouted, her voice devoid of yodel. Instead it was laced with fear, worry, and, by the look on her face, a large part anger. She rarely got mad, but when she did, look out.

"We—ah—" Ford stammered, blinking his eyes to adjust to the bright light of the entrance room.

"Ah, *Madame*," the English spy said in a perfect Parisian accent. "Your darling *enfants* merely lost their way. I do suggest you keep a very close guard on them for the rest of their time in Paris. This city does have a dark and dangerous side beyond the Catacombs."

Mom shook his hand. "Thank you for finding them. We won't let them out of our sight. *Merci*."

"Now, if you will excuse us. We must return to our posts," he said and then turned to the cousins, stepping close and lowering his voice. "Remember children. Listen to your parents, if you know what is best for you."

The American spy snickered and followed her partner towards the exit.

It was quiet. So very, very quiet. Bad sign.

"We can explain—" Ford began, but shrunk into himself under his mother's glower.

"Do not say one word," she said. "If you hadn't been found, you could have died."

"But Aunt May, we can explain. We were—" Ellie began.

"Sweetpea, you need to hush your mouth. You are in deep, deep trouble," Uncle Jim said. "Just march yourselves outside. We are heading back to the apartment."

Gavin remained silent, but caught Ford's eye. His face was as pale as Ford's after a vision. They had gotten so close to figuring out Great-Granddad's big mystery only to have Great-Granddad's box stolen from them. Ford couldn't help but feel like they had somehow let their great-grandfather down. And now their parents were livid. He glanced at his mom. She wouldn't even look at him.

Maybe Mme. Bellerose was wrong. Maybe Ford wasn't destined to do great things.

Ford dragged his feet as they stepped into the bright daylight. Dad pulled Gavin and Ford to the side, out of earshot of the rest of their family. "I am very disappointed in you two. Really and truly. Suffice it to say, you are grounded for the rest of our trip."

"Grounded? But Dad—" Gavin began.

"No, Gavin. I won't hear excuses and I am doubly disappointed in you. Quite honestly, I am shocked that you would allow your younger brother and cousin to put themselves in so much danger. It was so irresponsible and I expected more from you. Much more."

"Dad, don't blame Gavin. It wasn't his idea, it—" Ford began.

"So you just went along with it, Gavin?" Dad asked.

"No, that's not how it happened," Gavin said, his pale face flushed bright red.

Dad shook his head. "I don't have the stomach for this right now. The thought of losing all three of you in the Catacombs...just get on the bus. We'll talk about this when we get home."

Silence enwrapped them as the Whitaker-MacKenzie family trudged onto the bus.

Ford looked at Ellie. She winked back. What was she up to?

CHAPTER 39

The cousins had been under tight surveillance since the moment they got home. Dinner was one lecture after another about personal safety, risky behaviour, irresponsible decisions, and of course the resulting serious consequences. Mom ranted about "loss of trust" for a solid twenty minutes before Aunt June took over. They were dead serious about grounding them. They would not be let out of sight for the rest of their trip. The only thing they were allowed to do solo was use the washroom.

Mom stood at the end of the hall, watching the trio slink out of the dining room. "Straight to bed."

Ellie slipped Ford a slip of paper as she passed him on the way to her bedroom. He slid the note into his back pocket and stepped into the bathroom. Locking the door, he unfolded it. The message was short and to the point.

> F
> *Meet me in my room once the parents are asleep. I have something VERY important to show you. Mission Great-Granddad Mystery may NOT be dead!*
> E
> *P.S. DESTROY THIS NOTE!*

A thrill raced through Ford. All hope wasn't lost! That must have been what Ellie tried to tell him down in the catacombs. He tore the note into tiny pieces and flushed them down the toilet. If Mom or Dad caught them out of their bedrooms, their parents would totally lose it, but how much more trouble could they possibly get in?

CHAPTER 40

Ford yawned, then pressed his ear flush to his bedroom door. He hadn't heard any sound in the hallway for over an hour. He glanced at the clock on his desk. 12:22. Part of him wished he could just go to sleep. The vision today had drained him. If Ellie was right and she had found something that could help them, he couldn't just pull the covers over his head and ignore what could be their final crack at Great-Granddad's big mystery.

Ford gently laid his hand on the doorknob and slowly turned it. He stood still and listened. His heartbeat raced as he listened for sound in the hallway. Nothing. He opened the door a crack and peered out. The hall was dimly lit by the glow of the under-counter lights in the kitchen at the far end of the apartment. Holding his breath, Ford tiptoed next door to Ellie's room. Her door was slightly ajar, so Ford silently slipped inside her pitch-black bedroom. He stood for a moment to let his eyes adjust to the darkness. Gavin and Ellie sat on her bed, cross-legged across from each other. A tendril of déjà vu wafted over him as he neared them.

What was going on?

"Hey," Ford whispered. "So what's our last great hope?"

Ellie looked down at a piece of yellowed paper that lay on the bed between her and Gavin. Deep lines creased it. Ellie smoothed it out over and over, but it kept pulling up at the corners. Like lightning bolts, déjà vu coursed from it to Ford.

"This is it. Our last great hope. It's Great-Granddad's notes from the mission. I'm hoping it will hold one more of his visions. The moment I saw it in the wooden box, I thought it might be important. Luckily, I had already taken it when those stupid spies arrived. I shoved it into my pocket when they barged in."

"Well done, Ellie. I can feel something for sure. Loud and clear. It is definitely a keeper." Ford stared at the paper, not wanting to touch it. Yet. "What does it say?"

"You should read it yourself," Ellie said, holding it steady while Ford quietly read out loud:

Date: January 4, 1944

Mission Northern Lights
Lead Agent: Owl
Agent: Scout
Agent: Radley
Handler: Silver Fox

Last known location: Hotel du France, Rue.—
Secondary Interrogation Location for the Gestapo; confirmed use of torture

Confirmation of Owl's death—February 9th, 1944 by Wilhelm Müller

Confirmation of Scout's death—Nil

Errors: Failure of handler to remove agents; Mole in network—S.O.E. agent; Radley

<u>*Notes*</u>:
It is with great regret that I have failed in my mission to keep two agents in my network safe. Due to the sabotage of our mission by agent Radley, operatives Owl and Scout were arrested by German intelligence forces and handed over to the Gestapo for interrogation at the Hotel du France on Boulevard de Montmorency in Paris. After that, their trail went cold—they disappeared without a trace. They are gone. The loss of their young lives will forever be my cross to bear, throughout this lifetime and well into the next.

Silver Fox

Ford finished reading and looked at Ellie and Gavin. "Wow."

"Yeah and that's not all," Gavin said. "I searched up the double XX that was carved into the box lid and it is code for double agent."

Great-Granddad, a traitor. Ford couldn't believe it. "Double agent? Great-Granddad was a double agent?"

"Not exactly. At least we don't think so," Ellie said.

Date: January 4, 1944

Mission: Northern Lights
Lead Agent: Owl
Agent: Scout
Agent: Radley
Handler: Silver Fox
Last Known Location: Hotel du France, Rue. – Secondary
Interrogation Location for the Gestapo; confirmed
use of torture
Confirmation of Owl's death – February 9th, 1944 by
Welhelm Muller
Confirmation of Scout's death – Nil
Errors: Failure of handler to remove agents; Mole in
network – S.O.E. agent; Radley

Notes:
It is with great regret that I have failed in my mission
to keep two agents in my network safe. Due to the sabotage
of our mission by agent Radley, Operatives Owl and
Scout were arrested by German intelligence forces and
handed over to the Gestapo for interrogation at the
Hotel du France on Boulevard de Montmorency in Paris.
After that their trail went cold – they disappeared
without a trace. They are gone. The loss of their young lives
will forever be my cross to bear; throughout this lifetime
and well into the next.
  Silver Fox

"We know he was the handler for Owl and Scout, but we think he may have been a handler for other networks as well, which is why he had that notebook. Although again, we don't really have proof to support that theory. What we are pretty certain about is that no one would have all the information on the double agents. The way things were typically set up was one handler, or spymaster, would have the code names, another would know the agents' real names, and someone else would have had record of their missions, and so on. That way if one person was compromised it wasn't a catastrophic loss of security," Gavin explained.

Ford nodded. "So Great-Granddad's box was just one piece that MI6 or the CIA would need to find to figure it all out."

"Exactly, and Gavin found out that some of the missions during the war actually began years earlier and—" Ellie began.

"And they didn't necessarily stop when the war ended," Gavin interrupted, his words coming out in a flurry of excitement. He pushed his glasses up his nose. "In fact, there is strong evidence that indicates some of these missions are still underway today!"

Ford nudged Gavin over and sat on the bed. "What? Why?"

"After the war, the threat to the west shifted from Germany and its allies to Russia. There were some strong alliances with double agents that continued. They simply shifted the bulk of their attention from one enemy to a new potential threat—the U.S.S.R."

"Plus, spies have always existed. So it only makes sense for governments to want to use networks and contacts they already had in place," Ellie added.

"Geez. We really did uncover a landmine." Ford looked at the mission notes. "We need to tap into Great-Granddad's memories in there and find out more about his involvement."

Ellie reached over to her bedside table and grabbed her phone. "Exactly what we were thinking. No time like the present."

Ellie and Gavin climbed off the bed to give Ford more room. Ford tried his best to hide a yawn, but it was impossible. "Sorry. Tired."

"I wish we could all get some sleep, but our flight to London is tomorrow afternoon. We don't have any time to waste," Ellie said.

CHAPTER 41

Ford closed his eyes, his head lolled forward.

"Hey, don't fall asleep on us," Ellie said, shaking him gently.

"I don't think it would be possible to sleep through a vision," Ford replied, keeping his eyes closed.

"Are you ready, Little Brother?" Gavin asked.

Ford opened his eyes and nodded.

"Here you go," Ellie said and placed the note in his hand.

Ellie's darkened bedroom dissolved before Ford and Great-Granddad materialized. Ford had a strange sense that he had always been there, just out of sight, lost in time. Ford smiled. He sounded like Gavin.

Great-Granddad sat hunched over a wooden desk in a dingy apartment. Torn wallpaper hung in strips along one wall. He gripped a pen tightly in his hand.

Waves of emotion flooded from him to Ford. Ford's smile disappeared. "Great-Granddad is full of regret, fear, sadness, guilt," he murmured.

"My fault. My fault. I failed them," Great-Granddad dropped the pen and leaned forward, resting his forehead in his hands. "How did I not see this coming? How could I have been so blind to Radley's deception? Owl is dead, but Scout?" He stood and paced the room.

Ford gasped. "Great-Granddad is a disaster. He looks like he hasn't showered in a very long time, his face is covered in stubble, his hair is a greasy mess, and his shirt sleeves are stained and rolled to his elbows."

Great-Granddad ran his hand through his hair, leaving clumps standing on end.

"Who can I risk losing to save her? Who can I trust? If I ever get my hands on Radley..."

His angry words died out and he stopped pacing. He slowly shook his head. "There is no one," his words whisper quiet. "Am I just to leave her to rot in that hotel?"

He slumped on the bed. Tears streamed down his cheeks. "Scout, forgive me."

Ford sat up, jolted into the present. Great-Granddad and the broken-down room were gone. Ford blinked into the darkness. "We need to go there."

"Go where?" Ellie asked.

"To the hotel—the one the Gestapo used for interrogation. *Le Hotel du France* is the missing puzzle piece."

"Okay...but how? We are grounded, remember? How are we going to convince our parents that we need to stop by some random hotel tomorrow before we jump on a plane for England?" Gavin asked.

Ford yawned. "I am too tired to think straight. All I know is we need to visit the last place Scout was seen alive. My gut tells me that's where we'll find our answers."

Ellie jumped off the bed and grabbed her backpack from her closet. "Don't fall asleep yet." She rummaged around and pulled out a brown, squashed banana and a nearly flattened granola bar and tossed them one after the other onto her bed. "You need sustenance."

Ford pushed the smelly banana aside and ripped the wrapper off the bar. "Thanks," he mumbled, as he chomped.

"We need to call Marie-Claire," Ellie said. "She's our only option."

Ellie pulled her wallet out of her backpack and slipped out the business card that Marie-Claire had given them.

"Marie-Claire? Why?" Gavin asked.

"She likely has a car," Ellie replied.

"How is that going to help us? We can't just tell our parents that we are going for a ride with the friendly neighbourhood librarian. They won't buy it. Plus, as I keep saying, we're grounded. Possibly for life."

"We aren't going to tell them," said Ellie.

"What?" Ford asked, yawning, his eyes fluttering to a close. He was just seconds away from falling asleep sitting up. "I don't understand."

"We need to sneak out before they wake up. We need to get to the hotel and back to the apartment fast and to do that, we need a getaway car, hence we need Marie-Claire."

"So you think she is just going to drop everything and help us?" Gavin asked.

"Yes, I do." Ellie unplugged her phone from the charger. She entered the number Marie-Claire had given them at the library.

"Hi Marie-Claire," Ellie said as she typed. "We need your help. ASAP."

Ford gave into exhaustion and lay down, curling into a ball, his head on her pillow and his eyes closed.

"Marie-Claire," he murmured. "She's nice." And the world slipped away as he slid into a deep, dreamless sleep.

CHAPTER 42

"Ford, Ford," Ellie said, her whispered words invading his sleepy mind. "Time to get up."

Ford blinked his eyes open.

"You need to wake up. Marie-Claire is waiting for us downstairs. We have to go."

"Right." He sat up. "What time is it?"

"Four am," Gavin whispered. "You've been asleep for a few hours."

Ellie tossed Ford's hoodie onto the bed. "We think we have about an hour and a half. If we're back by 5:30, we'll be safe." She slung her backpack over her shoulder. "I've got everything packed. We snuck into the kitchen and restocked our Ford supplies."

Ford smiled. They made a perfect team. He swung his legs out of bed. "I'm ready."

Ellie eased the bedroom door open and Ford held his breath from the moment they stepped out of her room until they closed the apartment door. All three tiptoed down the hall until they reached the staircase, then broke into a run and raced down the stairs. Ford's sleep-fogged brain cleared more and more with every flight he descended and his mind now filled with a growing sense of urgency.

They burst out of the apartment block into the cool night air to find Marie-Claire dressed all in black, her hair tied back in a tight pony. She leaned against the side of a baby blue Fiat, looking like she had stepped off the pages of a *How to be an International Secret Agent for Dummies* book.

"*Bonjour, mes amis*," she said.

Ford's cheeks burned fire-hot as she kissed first one cheek, then the other. "Hi Marie-Claire. Thanks for helping us."

"Ah, *oui*." She embraced Gavin and finally Ellie. "It is my pleasure. I was very worried for you. You should have texted me sooner."

"Sorry," said Gavin. "We were just so…"

"Engrossed?" she offered.

"Yes, exactly."

"And now time is of the essence, yes? To solve the mystery of your *Great-Grandpère?*"

Gavin nodded. "Ellie texted you where we're going?"

"*Oui,* I have it in my GPS." She clapped her hands, like an elementary school teacher. "*Vite, vite.* In you get. Let us go. It is not a long journey by car."

She opened the door and Ellie and Gavin piled into the tiny backseat. Ford sat in the front with Great-Granddad's mission letter burning a hole in his pocket. At least that's what Ford imagined it was doing. Ford leaned back on the headrest and closed his eyes as Marie-Claire raced expertly down the dark and quiet streets.

Never before had any of Great-Granddad's items

retained any lingering memories. They had all been a one-time-only ticket into the past, but this note—it was different. It was like a phone that kept buzzing reminders of a missed call. This message from Great-Granddad kept sending him clairvoyant reminders of an important event, something Ford could not ignore. Ford knew in his heart there was more to this vision— more for him to see.

Marie-Claire whizzed around a roundabout. Dark buildings flew past. She raced through a second round-about, slowing only slightly. "We are making very good time. Traffic and the lights, they are on our side today."

"Thanks again for coming out so early in the morning," Gavin said.

"You are welcome. I would have come earlier, but I did not see your text right away. I am very...*curieuse*... curious by Ford and how he can see into the past."

They drove in silence for a few minutes down a wider street, before passing through yet one more roundabout. Once through, Marie-Claire took a sharp right and slowed the car to a stop.

"We're here?" Ellie asked.

"*Oui.*"

Ford stepped out of the car and stared at the large decrepit hotel. Great cracks ran up the side of the old building, most of the windows were boarded over. The sign over the door read, '*otel d Fran*'.

Ellie joined him on the sidewalk. "What a dump."

"Yes, it once was a lovely boutique hotel, but the war changed that. Once the Germans left, people didn't want to stay in a hotel the Nazis used for torture. Cursed by its history, twice the building was nearly destroyed by fire," Marie-Claire explained.

"Now it sits here boarded up and forgotten," Gavin said, standing on the other side of Ford.

"Forgotten. Just like the lives lost here," Ford murmured. He wandered to the side of the hotel, drawn to the narrow-gated alleyway that ran alongside. "This way." He led them through the open gate and down the alley to the back of the building. Fog rolled across his path.

He gasped. Something more than déjà vu nearly bowled him over. Goosebumps sprang to life across his arms.

"They're here. Owl and Scout. They're waiting."

CHAPTER 43

They looked around the overgrown garden. Grey mist oozed across the tall grass. Ford shivered in the cool air. A whiff of damp earth filled his lungs.

"How do you know they're here? Can you see them?" Ellie asked.

"I can sense—" Ford's words faded away as his gaze focused on a tall, bronzed monument partially hidden behind a cluster of trees in the centre of the garden. "What is that?"

Ford led the small party along a weed-covered cobblestone pathway that snaked around a maple tree and a clump of evergreens. With each step, the note in his pocket seemed to burn hotter and with more insistence. Ford's breath caught at the sight of the bronze figures of a woman in civilian clothes next to a uniformed man with a Labrador Retriever dog alert at his side.

"Jacques," Ford murmured. "It looks like Jacques."

"Here lie civilians and military alike, who gave their lives in a secret effort to end the atrocities of World War 2," Ellie read the inscription out loud, her voice breaking near the end of the sentence. She caught Gavin's eye. "We're in a cemetery?"

Gavin looked around. "I can't see any tombstones. Maybe they're hidden under the tall grass and bushes."

"It might not be an ordinary graveyard. This may be a mass grave site. If the Gestapo tortured and murdered people here, they wouldn't go to the trouble of giving them a proper burial," Ellie said.

"Allied Resistance" was etched in large letters across the base of the monument and Ford ran his fingers down the cool stone, tracing the word "Resistance." He pulled the note from his pocket and closed his eyes, letting his mind relax. He took a deep breath and slowly released it. His eyes fluttered open.

"This way."

He rounded the monument and took a few steps down another path. In shades of grey, partially hidden in the haze, there sat on a bench a woman with long hair swept up off her face and hidden underneath a tam.

"It's Scout. She's here."

Behind her stood a tall man in a long trench coat, a crooked grin on his face as he listened intently to her. Was this Owl? He fit the description. Scout tipped her head back and laughed—at least Ford assumed she was laughing. He couldn't hear either one of them. It was like watching a muted television show.

"Scout? Owl?" Ford called.

Scout cocked her head and frowned. She looked back at Owl who shook his head and looked around the cemetery.

Ellie, Gavin, and Marie-Claire stood beside Ford. He pointed to Scout and Owl. "Can you guys see them?"

All three shook their heads. Marie-Claire's eyes were as round as saucers. "You can see...people?" she asked.

Ford simply nodded.

"Afraid this is all up to you, but we'll be here. Just in case," Ellie said.

Ford's gaze returned to the two spies, who were busy in conversation. Ford still couldn't hear a word. A wave of déjà vu engulfed him and he gripped Great-Granddad's letter tighter, readying himself to revisit its memory, but the graveyard scene before him didn't vanish. It didn't even grey out or ripple the tiniest bit. In fact, nothing at all changed.

"Tom? Morah?" Great-Granddad whispered behind him.

An intense feeling, just like when he collided with his great-grandfather's soul, washed over him. It was like catching on fire from the inside out, but without the pain. Just heat as hot as the sun. Dizzy, he leaned on the bronze dog for support. The grass, cobblestone path, canopy of trees—flickered like an old fluorescent light bulb. He froze. Something was emerging between the flickers. No, that wasn't quite right. Someone was emerging.

Great-Granddad.

A far older version of his great-grandfather solidified before him—the old man Ford knew from his grandparents' wedding photos walked around the statues. Ford stumbled after him.

"Tom? Morah?" his great-grandfather repeated, this time his voice crisp and clear.

Morah rose from the bench and walked silently towards them. Tom followed, his face a mask, devoid of emotion.

"Silver Fox—Ed? Is that you?" Morah asked.

Finally, Ford could hear her.

His great-grandfather nodded, his eyes welled with tears. "I've waited so long to tell you, I am sorry. So very sorry," he said.

Morah gathered him into her arms as he sobbed.

Tom stood close, gripping Great-Granddad's shoulder. "The war is over, old man. It is over. Now you're home."

Great-Granddad withdrew from their embrace and sat on the bench.

"I am so deeply sorry. There is so much I regret. So much I wish I had done differently. The truth is, I should have known about Radley. I should have listened to your suspicions, Morah," he said, his voice a raspy whisper.

"We'll have none of that, shall we Tom?" Morah said, plunking down next to Great-Granddad. "We knew what the risks were, old chum. We knew what was at stake. That's the real truth."

"And the mission was far more important than any of us. Even you, Ed. Even more important than your regrets, and that is the rub, isn't it? War is hell for those who die and for those who survive. I wonder, who would count themselves luckier, the living or the dead?" Tom said.

Great-Granddad shook his head. "Who knows? Surviving after losing you both was...painful and you need to know," Great-Granddad's voice broke. "I never considered you throwaways. No matter what our directives were, neither one of you was expendable—at least not to me."

"We know," Morah said.

Tom nodded.

Great-Granddad frowned. Ford thought he looked confused. "So, where have you been all these years?"

Morah's eyes widened as she glanced at Tom. He stroked his moustache and shrugged.

"You don't know?" Scout asked.

Ford staggered closer. His head swimming. His heart raced. "Great-Granddad doesn't know he's dead. The truth shall set you free," he murmured. "He needs to hear the truth."

"Ford, are you okay?" Gavin asked, grabbing his arm, tugging him away from the bench. "You don't look so good."

"I'm fine, I'm fine," Ford said, frowning at his brother. "Wait. How can I see you in the middle of a vision?"

"I don't know," Gavin said.

Ford pulled free from his brother's grip. "They're here—all three, talking. Great-Granddad's so full of remorse. I need to…" his words drifted off as he neared his great-grandfather. He wanted to touch him. See if he could make contact. "Great-Granddad," Ford said, stepping closer.

His great-grandfather startled and frowned. He stood and squinted directly at Ford, his nose an inch away. His aura blasted out of him in waves, crashing into Ford. Ford stumbled two steps backwards, fighting hard not to fall.

"Who's there?" Great-Granddad asked.

"It's me," Ford replied. "Your great-grandson."

Great-Granddad looked across the garden.

"Ed, what's wrong?" Morah asked.

"I'm not sure. Is someone here?" He stepped towards Ford, but looked right through him. "Show yourself," he said, his voice a low growl.

Ford's heart raced. Nothing in the world seemed as important as connecting with his great-granddad right now. "I'm here, Great-Granddad. I'm right here."

Great-Granddad stepped back. "Did you hear that?" he whispered to Morah. "A voice."

She shook her head and Tom stepped closer to her. They both looked ready to fight.

"I'm here," Ford said and reached his hand to his Great-Granddad. It trembled like a leaf in the wind.

Great-Granddad extended an elderly shaking hand out in front of him, mirroring Ford.

Their fingers touched.

Warmth engulfed Ford.

Great-Granddad staggered backward, his eyes wide. "Who are you?" he whispered.

Ford smiled.

"I'm Ford, your great-grandson."

CHAPTER 44

Great-Granddad removed his glasses and rubbed them on his shirt. He pushed them back on and examined Ford's face. Was he looking for a resemblance? "You are my great-grandson, and I am long since dead?"

"Yeah, you died something like forty-five years ago, when my mom and aunt were little."

"Huh." Great-Granddad stared off into the distance, his hands folded in his lap.

"You didn't know?"

"No...I-I didn't."

Ford looked over his shoulder at Tom and Morah, who whispered to each other. Why couldn't they see him? What must they be thinking? Their long-lost friend suddenly appears, begs for forgiveness, and then parks himself on their bench and has a conversation with someone they couldn't see. Did they think Great-Granddad was speaking to a ghost? But weren't Scout and Tom ghosts? What did that make—

"Hello, Ford?" Great-Granddad said, bringing him back to the present.

"Sorry, it's just a lot to take in."

"Yes, it truly is. If I am dead and we've never met before today, why are we both here? What is this all about?"

"That is a very long story. Your other great-grand-kids are here too: Ellie and Gavin. I wish you could see them. They're standing over there, by the monument," Ford pointed at them huddled together. Great-Granddad frowned. Likely, none of this was making any sense to him. "It's all pretty complicated, but I can see into the past and see your old memories. Ellie and Gavin helped figure out your war history and together we used your memories to retrace your steps during 1944 and that led us here, to Morah and Tom. I think, after you died, you got lost somehow."

He nodded, his brows knit further. "You led me to Morah and Tom..." he said slowly "...so I could make amends." Great-Granddad cocked his head and smiled at Ford.

"Yeah, I guess so. That makes sense. And I have some bad news about the box you hid at the Catacombs..."

Great-Granddad leaned towards Ford, "Yes?"

"Uhm, well you see," Ford paused. How was he going to tell him that after all these years his own family had failed him, that he had failed him?

"Just say it, Ford. I'm already dead, how bad could it be?"

"MI6 found it," Ford blurted. "And it was our fault. We were so caught up in finding the box and figuring out what your great mystery was that we didn't realize we'd been followed into the Catacombs. The agents threatened Ellie and Gavin and I didn't want them to get hurt. So the real truth is, it's my fault. I gave the spies your box. I'm sorry."

Great-Granddad sighed. "Don't you worry about it. I knew it was a long shot and keeping those missions and agents safe for decades is far more than I had hoped for."

"So you're not mad?"

He laughed. "Impossible. You know, you have a tremendous gift."

"Yeah, it's tremendously weird."

"I wouldn't call it weird. Your gift found me and saved me—a dead man. To me, that sounds like a miracle."

"There's something I've been wondering about. In your box, we found a metal tube with negatives inside. Was that important?"

"Ah, yes, the dead-drop spike. I meant to plant that in the Champs-Elysées gardens for Radley, but of course that was prior to uncovering his betrayal. The contents of that spike are best left in the past." Great-Granddad flickered and dimmed. "I have to go now."

Ford's breath caught. "Can't you stay a bit longer? I have so many other questions." He wanted more time to talk.

"I'm afraid not," Great-Granddad said, standing. "It's my time to go. I have waited decades for this moment. Ford, you have my eternal gratitude."

Great-Granddad began to fade and the years seemed to slip away as well. He grew younger and younger until he looked like the man from Ford's visions. Tom slapped Great-Granddad on the back. He laughed, turned his head, and winked at Ford. Morah linked her arm through his and he turned to her and began to sing an old wartime song.

"We'll meet again, don't know where, don't know when. But I know we'll meet again some sunny day…"

All three continued to sing as they walked away across the garden, the fog swirling around them as they faded into nothing but memory.

"He's gone," Ford murmured, turning to face Ellie, Gavin, and Marie-Claire. A slow smile spread across his face. "We did it! We saved him from an eternity of guilt. That was our mission. Owl and Scout were waiting for him so he could make amends. And they weren't even angry. Can you believe it? They died and they weren't even angry."

His stomach growled. Loudly.

"Time to eat," he said, then collapsed to his knees.

CHAPTER 45

"Ford, can you walk?" Gavin asked.

"I dunno," Ford replied, trying to blink away his swirling vision.

"You take one arm, I will take the other and we shall help him to the car," Marie-Claire said.

"We are so late!" Ellie said, glancing at her watch. "It's already 5:07! We need to hurry." As fast as they could, they raced through the garden, down the narrow alley, and into the front street to Marie-Claire's Fiat. Gavin flopped Ford onto the front passenger seat and buckled him in, then squeezed into the back next to Ellie.

Ford groaned as nausea rose up his throat.

"You need to eat, Wizard," Ellie said, handing him a bunch of green grapes. "We can't have you fainting on us. We need you in top form so we can spring up those stairs at the apartment block."

She was right. If they didn't get into their bedrooms before Mom woke up, they would literally be grounded until they were forty. Ford popped two grapes in his mouth as Marie-Claire peeled away from the curb, making a fast U-turn in the middle of the street. They drove over the curb on the other side, never slowing.

"Hold on tight, *mes amis*. We are going to fly like the wind," she said, laughing. Ford held onto the door handle to brace himself as they flew down the street. The grapes on his lap flew to the floor as he rocked from side to side, around the corner and through traffic circle after traffic circle. The sky was brightening. Sunrise was moments away.

"We are almost there!" Gavin said. "I'm sure you can slow down now!"

Marie-Claire winked at Ford. "Your brother is a little bit of a scaredy-cat, yes?"

"He is a little protective."

She smiled as she pressed on the brakes. "As it should be. And we are here."

Ford unlatched his buckle. "Will we see you again?"

Marie-Claire shook her head. "Not likely. I am off to work in a few hours and you fly to England this afternoon, but we shall stay pen pals on the internet, yes?"

"That would be great," Ford replied, trying hard to stop his yawn, which proved impossible.

"*Au revoir*, Ford. It was my pleasure to meet you. I do not know what I just witnessed, but I feel in my heart that it was important," she leaned over the console and kissed him lightly on one cheek and then the other. "Stay safe, *mon ami*."

"Yes, yes, I will," he replied. He looked over his shoulder at Ellie and Gavin.

Ellie rolled her eyes. "Just for clarification, your eternal love was not what is important in her heart."

CHAPTER 46

Ever so quietly, Ellie turned the key in the front door of the apartment. Slowly, she turned the handle and pushed the door open, wincing as it creaked. She stood still and looked down the hallway. The coast was clear. Ellie stepped inside the still dark apartment, with Gavin behind her, guiding Ford.

Without a sound, Ellie closed the door and the trio tiptoed towards their bedrooms. Gavin led Ford to his room and gently helped him sit on the end of the bed, as he pulled back the comforter. Ford's blinks grew slower, his eyelids growing heavier.

"Time for sleep," Gavin whispered.

"Thanks," Ford mumbled as he crawled to the top of his bed and collapsed onto his side. Gavin pulled the soft comforter up to his chin.

"Sleep well, Little Brother."

Ford smiled, but he couldn't open his eyelids.

"You too…"

CHAPTER 47

Ford stretched and slowly opened his eyes. Streams of daylight cascaded into his room. He glanced at his clock. 1:15. He had slept past noon—way past noon—a record for him. Apparently, lack of sleep and a week full of Great-Granddad visions gave Ford sleeping superpowers.

Great-Granddad.

Ford sighed. Completing their mission felt bittersweet. Great-Granddad sure looked happy to be reunited with his friends, but life would be boring now.

He threw off his covers, swung his legs out of bed, and stumbled out of his room. Following the sounds of voices and laughter, he wandered down the hallway into the living room.

Dad looked up from his newspaper and smiled. "Well, look who finally decided to join us."

"Good morning, son," Uncle Jim said, ruffling Ford's hair.

"Looks like sleep agrees with you," Aunt June said.

"I should say so," Mom said, her voice tender. "You look better than you have since we arrived. That jetlag sure took some time to clear, didn't it?"

"Yeah," Ford said, looking at Ellie and Gavin.

Ellie smirked. "That jetlag is a beast."

"You'll need to grab a quick bite and jump in the shower. Our cab arrives at four o'clock to take us to the airport. You're one lucky young man. Ellie packed your bag for you while you slept," Mom said.

"No need to thank me," Ellie said. "Payment can be made in Euros or Pounds Sterling—your choice."

Ford ran a hand through his hair. "I am confused. Aren't we in trouble? Yesterday you grounded us, but today you're acting like everything is perfectly normal."

Mom laughed. "Oh, Fordie, you know we don't stay mad for long. Forgiveness is one of our most redeeming family traits."

"So true, MayDay, but that doesn't mean we forget quite so quickly," Aunt June added.

Mom winked at her sister. "You are utterly correct, JuneBug. Forgetting is most definitely not one of our defining features. So kidoooooos, we'll be waaaaaaatching!"

CHAPTER 48

A cool, moist breeze blew off the Thames as Ford stood with his back to the railing of Tower Bridge, with Ellie on one side of him and Gavin on the other.

"Can you believe we are in London?" he said, through clenched teeth. His jaw ached from smiling nonstop for the past half hour. His lips started to twitch.

"Just one more," Aunt June said, taking a few steps backwards. "I need to get the Tower of London in the background. It is the perfect backdrop for our first picture in jolly old London Town."

Ellie crossed her arms. "Mom, come on! You've taken a hundred shots already. Surely one of them is a keeper."

"Sweatpea, don't you rush your mom through this moment. If she needs to take 200 or even 300 more pictures, you will smile as sweetly as you can in every single one."

Ellie sighed. "Fine." She plastered on a huge, cheesy grin. "Good?"

Uncle Jim laughed, "You are as pretty as a peacock in a fourth of July parade."

"Oh, Daddy," she said, laughing. "That doesn't even make any sense."

"Look here, everyone. The sun is at just the right angle. Now…say…cheese!" Aunt June said.

Click.

She checked her camera display. "That's it! We're through. Now let's head to the Tower. I cannot wait to get inside that old fortress. There will be endless photo opportunities."

"Oh, joy," muttered Ellie.

Gavin laughed. "Hey, I told Mom and Dad about university last night and you were right, Ford. They were pretty cool about it."

"I told you," Ford said as they walked across the bridge. He frowned and stopped at the railing to stare at the Tower.

"What's wrong?" Gavin asked.

"Nothing is wrong, exactly…"

Ellie slid off her sunglasses and stared at him from under the brim of her baseball cap. "Then what's up?"

Ford smiled.

"I feel like I've been here before."

The End

ACKNOWLEDGMENTS

The idea for *Family of Spies* has bumped around my imagination for over ten years. In fact, I recall discussing my grandfather's mysterious war years with a table of writers at my first Society of Children's Book Writers and Illustrators Conference in Los Angeles in 2007. However, the seed of the story was planted when I was only a child by my mom, Bonnie Neil (Crawford). Every time she told and retold stories of her father and rumours of a connection to Sir William Stephenson, Canada's most famous spy, my imagination took flight. To put is simply: I owe her this book.

Every novel requires research, and with *Family of Spies* it was extensive and varied: from gathering facts about Britain's Special Operations Executive missions to 1940s slang; mapping the Paris Catacombs to finding floor plans of the Eiffel Tower; and even sorting out my grandad's relatives. Our family historian, Jim Crawford of St. John's Newfoundland, ensured I kept all the Henry and Harry Crawfords straight. My deepest gratitude to Jim, for the photographs, newspaper articles, answering my innumerable questions, and giving me access to his carefully built family tree. It feels like coming full circle that in order to write

Family of Spies, I had to return to Grandad's roots in Newfoundland.

This novel would not have been completed if it weren't for my writing group, The Streamers, from Hertford, England. Although I lived in Hertford for less than two years, I made friendships that will last a lifetime. Louise Morriss and Alice Hemming of The Streamers kept me writing at a fevered pitch and through invaluable critiques; they helped me wrangle my words into a solid plot. Together we have finished seven novels, and as of this moment, three of our books are under contract for publication. Three cheers for The Streamers! Hugs to you both!

"Don't judge a book by its cover." Wouldn't it be delightful if that old adage was true? In reality, a book cover is EVERYTHING and middle grade readers are no exception to that rule. I was fortunate to meet with Margaret Saull of McNally Robinson Booksellers, who offered her advice on book covers that entice and engage readers. Thank you, Margaret!

Yellow Dog has been a joy to work with and I am grateful they allowed me be actively involved with the design of *Family of Spies*. A massive thank you to Stephanie Berrington for her editorial insight and profound ability to perform "The Ruthless Edit." You killed my darlings so well that it hardly even hurt.

Relish Design, I am absolutely in love with the cover. Thank you for your beautiful work on both my Great Plains books.

From the very beginning, I wanted to have illustrations in *Family of Spies*, and Jamie Gatta's pen and ink drawings are even better than I had envisioned. Thank you Jamie, for saying "yes" and adding a visual element to *Family of Spies*.

To my family; Drew, Emma, and Sarah. Thank you for allowing me to discuss my characters as if they were real people and letting me bounce story ideas off you. And thank you for not holding me to promises I made while in the writing zone and only half listening. All my love, xoxoxo. P.S. Another book means another fancy dinner out to celebrate!

AUTHOR'S NOTE

Family of Spies is loosely based on the mystery revolving around my Rhodes Scholar grandfather, Edward Hugh Martin Crawford. He was a pilot with the R.C.A.F. and was awarded an MBE, based on his involvement in World War 2. Eighty years later, the details of his military career remain sealed. Our family lore of code breaking, secret missions, and connections to Bletchley Park, fueled my imagination when writing this story.

Family of Spies blends truth with imagination. Please check out Jodi's website at www.jodicarmichael.com to see where fact met fiction.

ABOUT THE ILLUSTRATOR

Jamie Gatta is currently an Educational Assistant for Pembina Trails School Division. He is a freelance illustrator and graphic designer who studied fine arts at the University of Manitoba and Production Art at Manitoba Institute of Trades and Technology.